'Let us not waste any more time with distracting trivialities. We need to talk seriously.'

'Yes, I know that.'

She wouldn't look into his eyes, she vowed nervously. Leandro Reyes was possessed of the kind of eyes that *stole* a woman's soul and haunted her for ever, and she needed to stay strong and focused—not just for her own sake, but for Raphael's too.

'You realise that you are going to have to agree to be my wife?' he said commandingly, before he leant back in his chair and sighed heavily. 'Don't you?'

The day **Maggie Cox** saw the film version of *Wuthering Heights,* with a beautiful Merle Oberon and a very handsome Laurence Olivier, was the day she became hooked on romance. From that day onwards she spent a lot of time dreaming up her own romances, secretly hoping that one day she might become published and get paid for doing what she loves most! Now that her dream is being realised, she wakes up every morning and counts her blessings. She is married to a gorgeous man, is the mother of two wonderful sons, and her two other great passions in life—besides her family and reading/writing—are music and films.

Recent titles by the same author:

THE PREGNANCY SECRET
THE MEDITERRANEAN MILLIONAIRE'S MISTRESS

THE SPANIARD'S MARRIAGE DEMAND

BY
MAGGIE COX

MILLS & BOON®

First published in Great Britain 2007
Harlequin Mills & Boon Limited,
Eton House, 18-24 Paradise Road, Richmond, Surrey TW9 1SR

© Maggie Cox 2007

ISBN-13: 978 0 263 19560 6
ISBN-10:   0 263 19560 0

Set in Times Rc
07-0107-47272

Printed and bou
by Antony Rowe Ltd, Chippenham, Wiltshire

THE SPANIARD'S
MARRIAGE
DEMAND

PROLOGUE

THE sun on the back of Isabella's head was like a laser beam of burning heat. Forced out of the stupor of her shocked thoughts by the discomfort, she got up from the couch and pulled down the fashionable bamboo blinds at the window behind her to introduce some much-needed shadow into the room. Summer had hit the UK with a vengeance and the pavement outside was hot enough to double up as a griddle. But even as she padded barefoot across the cool laminate flooring to return to the couch all Isabella could really focus on was the astounding revelation that she was pregnant. The results of the pregnancy test she'd just done, plus the tiredness and nausea she'd been suffering from for over a week now, were incontrovertible. Of all the unbelievably reckless, heart-stopping situations she could have returned from her trip abroad to face, this was one cataclysmic scenario she hadn't foreseen.

Trying to calm the throb of panic and wave of sickness that added to her already escalating anxiety, she leapt up again from her seat and fled to the bathroom. Ten minutes later, a cup of soothing chamomile tea at her elbow and a cool washcloth applied to the back of her heated neck, Isabella reviewed her situation with an acceptance and determination that stunned even her. Her passionate interlude with a handsome and famous son of Spain had resulted in her finding herself pregnant with his child. As she stoically assured herself she had all the necessary resources to cope alone and cope well she forced herself to resist the deep river of fear that was underlying her determined optimism, threatening to wreck everything. An ache for him—an earnest, bone-deep, silent plea that had surfaced before when she'd had to say goodbye to the man who had 'interrupted' her trip with the most profound impact—suddenly re-instated itself deep in Isabella's core and she knew even then…it would probably be her companion for the rest of her life.

CHAPTER ONE

May 2004—The Port of Vigo, Northern Spain.

'No! I don't care what you say to me or even if you never speak to me again, Emilia, but I'm not going to break off my own research for my book and hare off to God only knows where in pursuit of some surly, ego-centric film director who may or may not be where you say he'll be and most certainly wouldn't give me an impromptu interview even if I professed to be dying!'

Sucking in a deep, irritated breath following her passionate tirade to her sister over the phone, Isabella tapped her fingernails impatiently on the hotel reception desk where she'd taken the call and sensed a trickle of sweat meander slowly down her back. It felt like warm glue. It might be raining yet again but the dead heat was relentless. Right now she'd sell her soul for a cool shower and a cold drink followed by a lie down in her very plain but peaceful little room to gather her thoughts and perhaps catch a nap before doing some work. She'd been walking all day interviewing pilgrims on the famous route to Santiago de Compostela. Her back ached and her feet hurt but she was buoyed up by the companionship and enthusiasm of the pilgrims and after a rest was eager to get some writing done for her book. What Isabella most certainly *didn't* want was to fly off on some wild-goose chase in search of a man who apparently protected his privacy with the same level of heightened awareness and suspicion that security at international airports applied to their passenger checks these days. All because her beseeching, impulsive and ruthlessly ambitious sister saw an opportunity for an exclusive for her magazine.

'Please, Isabella…you can't *not* do this for me! You're right in the Port of Vigo in the same damn town as Leandro Reyes on the one and *only* day he's there on a speaking engagement and I'm pleading with you to do me this one huge favour! What do I have to do to convince you? Look… I'll pay you any amount of money you want…just name your price.'

'For goodness' sake, Emilia! I don't want money! All I want is to be left alone to get on with my trip in peace!'

Her sister's desperation was getting ridiculous, but then Emilia was hardly used to being denied anything. She was definitely the blue-eyed girl in their family. Three years younger than Isabella, she was the result of their mother's marriage to Hal Deluce—an amiable American she had met on a cruise round the Bahamas that she'd taken a year after Isabella's own father had died. Consequently Emilia had been credited a 'wonderful omen of better things to come' and since the day of her birth could do no wrong. On the other hand, a lot of unfair expectation had been laid on Isabella's shoulders simply because she was the eldest...expectations that she'd ultimately always known she would fail. An expensive wedding financed and arranged by her parents being a case in point. Isabella hadn't been able to go through with that particular scenario because she'd discovered at the eleventh hour that the relationship she'd had with her fiancé had been a complete and utter sham.

In contrast, the words 'failure' and 'Emilia' would never be used in the same sentence as far as her parents were concerned. Along with her thriving career as a journalist on one of the top-selling woman's magazines, she had married a handsome young stockbroker from a family who were practically landed gentry and had recently cemented her unchallenged position as 'she who can do no wrong' by moving into a rather grand house in Chelsea, where she rubbed shoulders with some of the glitterati she wrote about in her magazine. In their mother's view, their youngest had definitely 'arrived', whilst Isabella was still travelling.

Philosophical about it because she had to be, Isabella still couldn't deny that sometimes it hurt to be the one that hadn't quite 'made it'. And, because of her high standing in the family, sometimes Emilia's demands on the generosity and good nature of those who cared about her could almost border on the totally unreasonable. Like now—when she knew that Isabella was in Northern Spain specifically to research her book and meet the challenge of a five-hundred-mile pilgrimage covering from fifteen to twenty miles a day on foot over Northern Spain's dusty mesas. She wasn't on holiday or pursuing something 'frivolous'…she was working as well as walking.

That was not to say that Isabella didn't totally love what she was doing. Right now researching the Santiago de Compostela and why people sought to undertake the five-week-long trail, and actually walking it herself—she was in seventh heaven. That was why she didn't want to get distracted by something like this totally unexpected telephone request from Emilia.

'Don't you understand, Em? I'm working! I've taken a three-month career break from the library to do this and I don't want to waste even a second. I've been hiking all day, it's hot, I'm tired, I've got blisters on my feet the size of sumo wrestlers and I need to get some rest before working on into the night and walking again tomorrow. You're a resourceful woman—if you found out that Leandro Reyes is in Vigo today then I'm sure you can manage to find out where he'll be tomorrow! I'm sorry, but I can't help you…I really can't.'

There was a deep frustrated sigh at the other end of the line that spoke volumes. It said, If you don't do this for me then it proves you've let this family down again. It also said, I thought you were my sister? I thought you *cared* about me? Now I can see that you obviously don't.

A stab of unhelpful guilt wove its nefarious way down Isabella's already suffering spine and she bit her lip to stop herself from automatically changing her last statement to a more agreeable one.

Stealing an agitated glance at her watch, she lifted her eyes to the small, winding stone staircase where her plain, peaceful room tantalisingly beckoned. She hadn't even unpacked her rucksack yet. She'd been about to do just that when she'd had the call from Emilia. Isabella had given all the phone numbers of where she'd sometimes be staying ahead of her travels to her mother. That was on the odd occasion when she was staying in small cheap hotels and not the *refugios* and monasteries widely used by the pilgrims. Now after this call from her sister, Isabella had cause to wish she'd told *nobody* in her family where she would be.

'I'd sell my house to get any information I could on Leandro Reyes, Isabella! When I found out from Mum that you were due in the Port of Vigo today I got so excited! I only heard last night that he was going to be there and I've got several crucial meetings lined up this afternoon or else I would have flown out there to try and see him myself. It's too late now even if I could get a flight…as far as I know he's only planning on being there for the evening. This means so much to me, sis…to my career. Leandro Reyes is a *God* amongst art-house film directors! Most feature writers would sell their soul to interview him! Please try and get to meet him… please! Even if you get only one or two sound bites it wouldn't matter. At least you'd get some good impressions of the man himself that I could embellish for the magazine!'

Isabella's heart sank. Emilia worked for a supposedly respectable upmarket glossy, but they still weren't above 'dishing the dirt' on a star or a celebrity if the opportunity arose. That kind of sensationalist tabloid journalism was despicable in Isabella's opinion. She knew it was naïve, but couldn't they leave these people alone? Everyone was entitled to some privacy...even much-lauded and sought-after film directors, in her opinion. *Especially* ones like Leandro Reyes who—she'd heard somewhere or another—had a reputation for being almost spectacularly reclusive and enigmatic. Her heart bumped a little at the idea of even being in the same sphere as a man like that—never mind trying to get him to talk to her! Swallowing over the dryness of her parched throat and quite desperate for a drink, Isabella caught the curious gaze of the elderly plump Spanish matriarch bedecked in black behind the small reception desk and politely smiled. 'I have to go now, Emilia. I need a shower and a drink and then I—'

'I'm begging you, Isabella! Leandro will be at the Paradisio. It's one of the more discreet places in the Port and he's meeting a colleague there for a drink.'

'I suppose I'm wasting my time asking you *where* you get your information from?'

'If you must know I was at a film première last night and at the party afterwards I overheard a conversation between a couple of Americans in the film business who'd just done some work with Leandro. They happened to mention that he had a speaking engagement today at a local college and was meeting a mutual friend of theirs afterwards in the Port of Vigo for drinks. He'll be there from seven o'clock onwards. Ring me at home tonight after you've seen him. I'll wait up to get your call. Thanks, sis...you're an angel! I knew I could count on you!'

'Don't you know that it's not ethical to eavesdrop on other people's conversations?'

'Oh, get real, Isabella! You and your high-minded principles!'

Letting that comment ride, Isabella lifted up some hair from the back of her heated neck where it coiled damply in silken black strands. 'But how will I know what he even looks like?' Reclusive art house directors weren't photographed with the constancy of someone like Stephen Spielberg, Isabella was sure.

'He's six foot one of pure trained muscle with dark hair and eyes the colour of polished slate and not surprisingly the most sought-after bachelor in the business. Trust me…you won't be able to miss him!'

Before Isabella could draw another breath, the receiver at the other end was swiftly replaced and the line ominously hummed its disconnection signal in her ear instead.

As Leandro Reyes glanced round at the almost empty bar, the back of his neck crawled with slight unease. Alphonso should have shown up half an hour ago…that had been their arrangement. His fellow director and friend had wanted to meet urgently, he'd said, to discuss a project he had been offered and wanted Leandro's professional opinion on. When he'd discovered Leandro would be in the vicinity today—*en route* to his house in Pontevedra after his speaking engagement—he had suggested they meet at the Paradisio to talk. It was a quiet, out of the way place where no one would bother them and the owner of the small bar had promised to provide food if they were hungry. At the thought of food, Leandro's empty belly obligingly grumbled. He might as well sit it out until Alphonso finally showed his face—*if* he was going to show it at all—and in the meantime he could have something to eat and think about his own overloaded schedule for the next six months. A waiter appeared almost as soon as Leandro got to his feet and it left him wondering if the man had been spying on him. He smiled secretly at his own paranoia then placed his order for some seafood— something that the port restaurants and bars naturally excelled in.

'*Sí,* Señor Reyes. It will be my pleasure.'

'*Grazias.*'

Slightly inclining his head, Leandro made his way slowly back to the table he'd briefly vacated. An elderly man a few tables away from him looked up from his newspaper and smiled courteously. The edges of Leandro's mouth moved only infinitesimally upwards in a return gesture. He wasn't accustomed to giving his smiles easily. Glancing out through the arched stone windows that overlooked a small neat patio area with various plants dotted around—some better tended to than others—he noticed a woman approach in the twilight. Something about her seemed hesitant... unsure—as if she wasn't entirely certain that she had found what she'd been searching for. Aside from the fact that she was more than pretty enough to command his full attention, Leandro speculated on her reason for being there. Was she meeting her lover, perhaps? His stomach tightened with a surprising flash of jealousy at the thought.

As she came in through the opened doorway he saw

that her beguiling attractiveness pleasurably increased on close quarters. As far as he could tell, her eyes were dark as Columbian roast coffee—with long sable hair in a pony-tail to match—yet her complexion was surprisingly fair. Something told him that she was not Spanish. A tourist perhaps? She was dressed in faded jeans and a loose white shirt—not dissimilar to Leandro's own garb—and her presence brought a distinct breath of cool, fresh air into the small overheated bar. Waiting to be served, she frowned when the bar's owner did not immediately appear. Glancing round, she settled her somewhat anxious gaze with startling intent upon Leandro. He felt the impact of that searching gaze ignite a powerful little flame of want deep inside him—this time Leandro's smile was not so reticent.

Alphonso was either late or not coming at all and so what would it hurt to entice this raven-haired beauty with her big dark eyes into having a little conversation with him to help while the time away?

'The bar owner is busy,' he offered in flawless Spanish. Then, when she frowned, Leandro quickly deduced she didn't understand. 'Are you meeting somebody?' he asked, switching effortlessly to English.

'No…I mean…I mean perhaps.'

Twin circles of scarlet added fetching colour to her otherwise pale beauty. So she *was* a tourist…an English tourist since there was no trace of any other accent in her soft appealing voice. Leandro's attention was trapped as thoroughly as a lynx caught in a snare.

'You are unsure if you are meeting someone?' he asked teasingly.

'Not exactly…I mean…can I talk to you?' Lowering her voice, the intriguing young woman came nearer and with her brought the haunting scent of jasmine. *There are other things besides talking I would like to do with you, mi ángel…* Leandro thought silently, his senses unbelievably stirred as he considered her arrestingly pretty face.

'I—this is very awkward and I don't normally do this sort of thing, but…are you Leandro Reyes?'

*So…*she was not an 'innocent' tourist at all! Disappointment bit hard. She was either an opportunist actress looking hopefully for a chance to get into the movies—something that happened with more frequency than Leandro cared to catalogue—or else a reporter. Gut instinct told him it was probably the latter choice. What a pity! If he didn't dislike journalists with such a vengeance he would have been only too happy to entertain this beautiful young woman all night. As it was, he now saw her presence as a contemptible intrusion into his fiercely guarded privacy. How the hell had she found him here? He did not recognise her from amongst the students at the college he'd spoken at earlier today, so how had she discovered his whereabouts?

'That is not your concern,' he replied coolly, the shutters clearly coming down over his sensational silver-grey eyes.

At that moment Isabella could have strangled her own sister. What had Emilia persuaded her to do? She wasn't the type of person who intruded on anyone's privacy and even if she recognised someone famous in the street or in public somewhere, she'd be the last person to bother them! Now this Leandro Reyes—this esteemed film director who protected his privacy with a notoriously zealous verve—was looking at her as if she were a fly he would like to swat out of his eye-line!

'I'm really sorry if I'm bothering you—' Isabella unconsciously licked her upper lip to stop it from quivering '—but I truly meant no offence. I knew this was a bad idea but I'm afraid I acted against my better judgement. I should never have come over to you…please forgive me.' She turned away, her intention to leave this place as quickly as possible and put the embarrassing memory behind her. When she rang Emilia later on tonight she wasn't half going to give her a piece of her mind! She must have been insane to even *think* she might pull off such a thing as garner an interview with this man! She'd seen the disparaging glance he'd swept her with only too clearly. He'd probably been disturbed by unscrupulous journalists and reporters too many times to give them anything but the lash of his tongue—let alone an interview!

'Wait a moment.'

His voice, throaty and at the same time as richly beguiling as brandy warmed over a flame, halted Isabella in her tracks. 'What publication do you work for?'

'I don't.'

Turning round slowly again, Isabella looped some loose strands from her pony-tail behind her ear. The cool grey eyes of Leandro Reyes were surveying her with suspicion and deep mistrust. Just then Isabella would rather be stranded in the deep snows of Siberia than having to endure his terrifying scrutiny.

'What do you mean…you *don't*?'

'I mean I'm not a journalist myself. I'm in Spain researching a book I'm writing. And I only came to find you because my sister, who works for a—a women's magazine in the UK, rang me when she knew I would be here in the Port of Vigo the same time as you, Señor Reyes.'

'So it is your sister who wants to interview me for her magazine?'

'That's right. Once again, I can only offer my apologies for intruding like th—'

'How did she know that I would be here today? Where did she get her information from?'

How could she tell him that Emilia had overheard a private conversation? It would surely damn both her and her sister in his eyes. Isabella's desire to escape the scathing cynosure of this disturbing man grew almost unbearable even though she told herself his acute irritation was justified. Right now she should be back at the little hotel she was staying in, closeted in her room making notes from her talks with some of the pilgrims earlier today—not acting like some ill-equipped spy on behalf of her sister! This disturbing and unwanted encounter had totally set her back and it was going to take all her concentration to even write her name, let alone anything more challenging tonight!

'I'm sorry, but you'd have to talk to my sister about that. Please accept my apologies for disturbing you, Señor Reyes. I told my sister it was a bad idea at the time but she can be very persuasive…unfortunately.' Grimacing and slightly ashamed that she'd confessed as much, Isabella started to walk away again. Once more, Leandro stopped her in her tracks.

'So…you are a writer? Are you published?'

'No…not yet. At the moment I work as a librarian but it's always been my ambition to write books full time.'

'And this book you are working on…is it a work of fiction?'

For a moment Isabella was so mesmerised by the hypnotic concentration of this man's quixotic gaze that thinking was no easy feat. In fact, her thoughts felt like incomprehensible words on a Scrabble board that had been completely muddled up!

'No…it's not. I'm—I'm writing about the pilgrims who walk the Camino Way to Santiago de Compostela. My grandfather was Spanish, you see, and he told me so many stories about it that it's always been my ambition to come here and experience it for myself.'

Leandro found his temper irrevocably easing as he studied the girl in genuine surprise. The Camino de Santiago de Compostela—The Way of Saint James— was very important to him and his family—to *all* the people in this region of Northern Spain. Many had walked it in their turn and received blessings that they talked about to this day. Perhaps this pretty young woman with her soulful ebony coloured eyes and her milk-and-honey skin was not cut from the same cloth as those 'kill for a story' reporters that were sometimes a plague on his industry. Could it not be possible that she had more integrity than that? Leandro wanted to believe so even if his mistrustful nature advised against it. She had to possess *some* good qualities if she was writing about the Santiago de Compostela pilgrimage. Warring within himself to give her the benefit of the doubt, Leandro decided to relent—telling himself that he would find out soon enough if she was the genuine article or not.

'So…you are walking the Camino yourself?' he asked intrigued.

'Yes, I am…but I've also been stopping for a day or two at a time to talk to other pilgrims for research for my book and do some writing. I've heard some truly inspirational stories so far and I've got loads of wonderful material to work with!' Almost guiltily catching the full force of his piercing examining gaze, Isabella bore his investigation with mounting trepidation, then let loose a sigh. 'Anyway…I should go and leave you in peace. I have plenty of notes to write up and I must get on. I'm very pleased to have met you, Señor Reyes.'

'If that is true, then you should not be in such a hurry to leave…no?' He pushed the legs of the wooden chair opposite him at the table with one booted foot so that they scraped along the terracotta floor tiles towards her, making Isabella jump. Her cheeks flooded with heat and Leandro smiled at her with a lazily confident air that said he knew she would not think of refusing his invitation to stay. But inside Isabella was torn. Now that she'd got what she'd wanted—or what Emilia had wanted—the whole scenario had left her with a bad taste in her mouth and all she wanted to do was go back to the hotel and look over her notes. She also had a long day's walking ahead of her tomorrow and it was probably wiser to just get some rest.

'I... I'm sorry but I have to go.'

Emilia would kill her for blowing such an opportunity to talk to the enigmatic director but that was just too bad. She wouldn't impose on this man one second longer than she could help it, Isabella decided.

'What is your name?' Leandro asked her, seeing her sudden indecision.

'Isabella Deluce.'

'Isabella? Like our famous queen... Well, Isabella...' The way his tongue rolled the syllables of her name made it sound like the most shockingly intimate caress and she shivered almost violently. 'I will talk to you about the Camino and the pilgrimage, but my private and professional life are strictly out of bounds... Is that clear?'

Swallowing down her shock at his words, Isabella smoothed her hand nervously down the front of her jeans. 'Yes, of course...but you'd really talk to me about the Camino?'

'I have said so, have I not?'

Leandro's mercurial eyes skimmed down Isabella's body in her white cotton shirt and light blue jeans and lingered for a moment on the long, shapely legs that she had inadvertently drawn his attention to with her restless hand. He lifted his gaze back up to her flushed and lovely face with its arresting little dimple in her chin with undeniable satisfaction.

'Now come and sit down,' he ordered huskily, his tone allowing no opportunity for dissent. 'We will talk about the Camino and you can tell me some of your impressions so far. Have you eaten yet?'

'No…but I can easily get something when I return to my hotel.'

'Then please join me… I have already ordered some seafood and Señor Varez, the owner of the bar, will no doubt provide me with far too much to eat alone. I think we must also have some wine… I have found in my experience that wine definitely assists the conversation to flow.'

When Isabella still hesitated to take the chair Leandro proffered, his lips split into a wide provocative grin.

'Do not look so alarmed, pretty Isabella… I may look quite the pirate with my long hair and unshaven jaw, but I assure you that I do not intend to throw you over my shoulder and take you back to my cabin to ravish you…unless of course you have a secret desire that I do just that!'

CHAPTER TWO

ISABELLA found herself lowering her body into the sturdy wooden chair opposite Leandro with her limbs trembling—a small riot going on inside her at the fact that he had made such a disturbingly unexpected and risqué comment. Glancing into his now twinkling grey eyes and the surprising dimples either side of his sensual mouth, she remembered her sister's comment about him...

He's six foot one of pure trained muscle with dark hair and eyes the colour of polished slate.

Now she saw that even *that* description didn't do him justice. He was absolutely right. He *did* look a bit like a pirate—but a modern-day, rather bohemian one than his perhaps coarser counterpart from another century. And in spite of his casual clothing and long shoulder-length hair—indicative perhaps of a somewhat bohemian sensibility—Leandro Reyes also had an air of authority about him that said you'd be wrong to assume his morals or values were equally 'unconventional'.

Now that he'd insisted she stay and Isabella was actually going to have a conversation with him, she wished hard that she knew more about him. Her knowledge of his films or any of his other achievements was scant and that vaguely embarrassed her—even though Emilia had sprung this whole event upon her out of the blue. Isabella loved going to the movies and her leaning was definitely more towards the kind of thought-provoking films that directors like Leandro were famous for, but she'd never actually seen one of his films as far as she could recall. Like her beloved grandfather, Isabella's first love was books and, though it might have been a disappointment to them, it had been no surprise to her family when she'd opted to train as a librarian instead of something that carried a bit more professional kudos. And now, even though Isabella aspired to be an author, they clearly viewed this pursuit as a bit of a 'fool's mission' as well as being certain that she wouldn't make any money out of it.

'Now I have made you blush!' Leandro teased, clearly enjoying her apparent discomfort at his playfully taunting words. 'Have I embarrassed you, pretty Isabella?'

'No, Señor Reyes.' She shrugged. 'Well, yes…a little. I think I would just prefer our talk to be concentrated on the pilgrimage, if you don't mind.' Wanting desperately to divert his teasing because it would be the most disturbing distraction from his storytelling, Isabella tried to assume a more comfortable position in her chair. She also didn't want him to imagine that she was one of those easily flattered women who would welcome and even encourage his flirtatious remarks.

'Leandro…my name is Leandro and if we are to spend the evening together talking then I must insist that you call me that and *not* Senor Reyes…*sí*?' Before he could examine further the surprise in her distractingly alluring dark eyes, Señor Varez addressed him from the bar. He had a telephone call. Leandro didn't doubt that it was Alphonso explaining why he had been held up. Smiling at Isabella as he rose up from the table, he found he was no longer impatient for his friend to arrive...not now that he had a more interesting diversion. When he returned from taking the call only minutes later he shrugged as he lowered his tall, muscular frame back into his chair, his movements fluid and unhurried.

'My meeting is cancelled so now you may talk to me at your leisure, Isabella.' He leaned forward a little, his expression becoming serious. 'But just for the record— I would prefer it if what we discussed stayed just between us and did not get published in your sister's magazine. You may use what I say to help you with your book, but that is all. I have to have your utmost agreement about this otherwise we cannot proceed.'

'Of course...and thank you for agreeing to talk to me.'

To his complete surprise Leandro found that the prospect of spending the evening with this young woman was one that he definitely looked forward to, despite his cautious nature urging him to be careful of revealing too much—even inadvertently. Apart from her looks—which were a definite magnet—there was something about her that prompted in him a deep curiosity. And there was caution in her eyes too... Leandro recognised it. He wondered what or *who* had put it there. On the whole, she seemed a charming mixture of woman and child and he hoped he would not come to regret breaking with precedence by giving her a small window into his thoughts and beliefs about the Camino.

But apart from his undeniable fascination for his un-expected dinner companion, he was also concerned to hear from Alphonso that his wife, Perdita, had left him and that was the reason he had postponed their meeting. So many of his friends seemed to be having marital problems these days and frankly Leandro was glad not to have that particular issue dog his life. He was quite happy to be unattached and free from entanglement. Especially as the one and only time he'd fallen in love it had left him bruised and angry when his lover had betrayed him with another man, as well as fuelling his belief that once trust was broken it was almost impos-sible to regain it. One day he would marry—because a man should have children, as his father was always telling him—but right now Leandro's work came first. Film-making was his total passion and every day he thanked God that he was blessed with the good fortune to be able to make it his career. But that said…neither could he resist the demands of the hot Latin blood running in his veins. And, yes, beautiful intelligent woman *were* a potential weakness. Especially when they were as highly attractive as the sweet, dark-eyed *señorita* sitting opposite him…

Isabella told herself that she should be more concerned about writing up her notes and getting some rest this evening rather than talking to this surprising and fasci-nating film director. But she justified her staying put in her chair by telling herself she was bound to discover a wealth of useful information about the pilgrimage and the region by listening to this man. It would be absolutely invaluable for her research.

'So...you want to know about Santiago de Compostela?' Leandro smiled enigmatically and Isabella's muscles tensed in excited expectation.

'I would love to,' she replied softly, her eyes shining.

Time passed, and, fortified by a generous glass of the local Albarino wine and the biggest dish of shellfish Isabella had ever seen served anywhere, including the national delicacy, *pulpo*—Octopus—she found herself becoming thoroughly and effortlessly enchanted by the history and mythology of the area that Leandro revealed to her. He reiterated for her the popular belief that the bones of the apostle St James lay interred beneath the altar of Santiago's great Spanish Baroque Cathedral— hence the reason for the pilgrimage—and regaled her with some haunting tales of the *morriña*. The *morriña* was noted for being a particular kind of melancholic mood that could descend on people, and the wildly powerful Atlantic storms that took place in the region were regarded to be the main cause of it. It was something that the Galicians shared with the Celtic people of Ireland.

At the end of two hours, Isabella had written nothing down but had, hopefully instead, consigned most of Leandro's powerful stories about the Camino to memory. Meeting him had been an unexpected and exciting bonus to her trip and some part of her silently acknowledged that perhaps fate had taken a hand and steered her towards this man for a very good reason. She wouldn't be the first person to experience miracles on this pilgrimage—not by a long shot. Not once had Leandro spoken about himself, his family or his illustrious career and even though she realised he was actively guarding his privacy, Isabella was impressed that he apparently had no need to exercise his ego in that regard by heralding his triumphs. She could have listened to him for ever... His voice was like a warm, protective blanket tucked round her on a cold stormy night and was as compelling as his seriously haunting good looks and the deliciously long, slow glances he gave her that aroused and heated her blood with undeniable force. Isabella was more intoxicated by him than if she'd drunk a whole bottle of Albarino wine by herself. His exceedingly relaxed delivery of his stories was also deceptive because the passion in his voice was unmistakable. It suggested the kind of passion that a woman secretly craved and despaired of ever finding. A passion that spoke of excitement, discovery and, yes, danger too...and would undoubtedly be as strongly addictive as the most powerful opiate.

Just sitting listening to Leandro had made Isabella think about the polar opposite of feeling she had experienced with her ex-fiancé, Patrick. That was why—even though he'd let her down badly by commenting on the most intimate aspects of their relationship with a friend in a rather ribald manner that Isabella had unfortunately overheard—ultimately she'd known they had no future together. It was why, only two days before the wedding, she had finally decided against tying herself to such a disloyal man and realised she'd rather remain single for the rest of her life than risk a marriage that would leach all the joy out of her over time.

There was a sudden crash from outside as a powerful gust of wind upended a metal chair onto its side. The spell Leandro had woven around Isabella with his storytelling was abruptly broken by the harsh grating sound. As the forceful breeze roared louder and heavy rain started to pelt the cobbled streets like a downpour of small stones Isabella reluctantly reflected that she really ought to be getting back to her hotel. She was quite used to the frequent bouts of rain by now and getting drenched was not her biggest concern. At any rate she'd soon dry off when she got back to her room. Touching her napkin to her lips, she dropped it back onto her plate and reached for the canvas shoulder-bag she'd left on the floor beside her chair, willing time to stand still so that she could stay right where she was for ever and listen to Leandro relate more of his entrancing stories.

Glancing anxiously at the windows as Señor Varez hurried round closing the shutters against the noisy howl of the wind, Isabella bit down on her lip—a desperate hollow ache inside her at the thought that when she walked out of the door in a couple of minutes' time she would never see Leandro Reyes again.

Trying to hide her regret, she offered him a brief but grateful smile. 'I don't know how to begin to thank you for giving me such a valuable opportunity to talk to you, Señor Reyes—'

'Leandro,' her companion insisted with unapologetic

authority, his piercing grey-eyed gaze at that moment shredding her composure to bits as he concentrated it very intently on her. 'You are not leaving already? Apart from the fact that it is pouring with rain, you have barely told me anything about yourself! And I still do not know why you are walking the Camino… It is not just because of your book I am sure.'

He had known for a good hour or more that he did not want her to leave. He realised that he had commandeered most of the dialogue between them and now wanted to allow her to make up for the deficit, as well as powerfully desiring to extend the time they spent together. She was an unusual woman and Leandro felt his interest in her growing. Not once had she flirted with him or cast her eyes at him in a seductive manner, as most women given the opportunity to be alone with him would have. Especially knowing who he was.

To be honest, Isabella's lack of feminine response to him as a man had seriously started to perturb Leandro, because he was definitely experiencing some very powerful male stirrings as he continued to rest his gaze on her. At one point she had put her elbows on the table and rested her head in her hands as she'd listened enthralled to a story he'd told about a vision of an angel a friend of his had had whilst undertaking the pilgrimage, and her bewitching gaze had been so focused and enraptured that Leandro had almost lost the thread of his story. Privately he'd begun to examine the beguiling contours of her lovely face with increasing delight.

The wine he had imbibed had undoubtedly helped mellow his mood, but he had already decided before he'd even drunk half a glass that he would not continue on his way to his house in Pontevedra tonight. No, he would stay in Vigo and make his way home tomorrow morning instead. His plan was to take a couple of days out to read manuscripts and catch up with paperwork before travelling back to Madrid to embark on his next project.

The look Isabella gave him in return for his comment definitely seemed to demonstrate her surprise that he would want to have her talk about herself.

'I'm not bothered about the rain... I've got used to it. It's kind of you to be interested in my book, but, to tell you the truth, I've had a long day's walking,' she replied apologetically, 'and I was intending on making an early start in the morning. But thank you again for everything...for the food and wine and wonderful stories about the Camino.'

To his amusement and surprise she offered Leandro her hand. He glanced at it for only a moment before raising it to his lips and softly kissing the exquisitely satin skin that smelt so alluringly of jasmine. The hard muscled wall of his stomach tightened like an iron band encircling him as desire flared with the force of an incendiary and the heat it generated in him almost made him vocalise his pleasure out loud.

'As unexpected as it was, you have accorded me much pleasure with your company tonight, Isabella... truly. But perhaps we can rectify the fact that I have learned so little about you, hmm? I have decided not to make my onward journey home to Pontevedra tonight after all. There is already a storm outside and it will only get worse, I am sure—not the best conditions for driving in. I was going to suggest we go somewhere else for the night and continue our conversation there? A friend of mine has a place not far from here. I can make a phone call and get a car to pick us up. We can be there in no time.'

He was—according to Emilia—one of the most famous film directors in all of Spain and he was suggesting that Isabella go with him to a place owned by a friend of his and spend the night there? As she considered the hand he had just kissed with its still-electrifying impression of the warmth of his lips and the brush of his beard her mind seemed incapable of forming a reply.

'Isabella?'

In the absence of an answer, Leandro frowned, his high cheekbones and fascinating eyes leaving an indelible imprint on Isabella that she wouldn't relinquish in a lifetime.

'Yes?'

'I want you to spend the night with me…you understand?'

He could ask the question in a dozen different languages and, from the almost fierce, hot look in his electrifying gaze, Isabella could not fail to comprehend his meaning. The question was…what should she do about it? In some secret hopeful, delighted place inside of her the decision was already made. Yet still Isabella fought against the powerful heated undertow, terrified of being overwhelmed by it—of being too reckless and living to regret it… Not because she didn't desire Leandro—but because she desired him almost too much.

'I understand perfectly. But I'm afraid that can't be, Leandro.' She dipped her head, feeling her face flame red beneath his mocking examination. Surely her lack of sophistication would only amuse him? 'I'm here to walk the Camino. That really *has* to be my focus.'

At her unexpected, soft-voiced repudiation of his suggestion Leandro wanted Isabella even more. The wanting was akin to the slow, heavy heat that made a person tense and expectant for that heart-jolting crash of thunder just before a storm. In the end you longed for the release. That longing dictated that he *couldn't* let her go—that any move she made to put any kind of distance between them would have to be diverted because now he was determined to have her at all costs. His friend Benito's hotel was just a few kilometres away. The man was one of Leandro's oldest friends and implicitly understood his need for privacy. There would be no danger of the paparazzi getting wind that he was staying there. Leandro would have all night to seduce Isabella and enjoy her company. Now the idea had entered his head, it quickly became a fixation. 'I want you to come with me. Now that it comes down to it, I find I cannot let you go.'

As seductive and flattering as his declaration was, Isabella knew she could not simply succumb to his request because he had expressed it so forcefully. Did she really want to risk having her heart broken by this man? Because right now, from where she was standing, that was a distinct possibility. She'd never met a man who was so hard to resist and frankly it scared the daylights out of her. Especially so since she was still feeling vulnerable over the mistake she'd made over Patrick.

'I really *can't* stay, Leandro.' Isabella's throat tightened unbearably. 'I need to get back to my hotel before—'

'I do not accept that you cannot stay!'

He crushed her mouth beneath his own, in that blind, heated moment of desire, not caring that he might bruise her too tender lips or scratch her delicate skin with his beard-roughened jaw. All Leandro knew was that the need to touch her was a compulsion he could not resist… The need to feel her soft, womanly body in his arms and breathe in all the utterly feminine scents that threatened to make him slowly lose his mind was the one driving imperative that he could not ignore. Isabella had been driving him slowly crazy with want, all evening. When he finally and abruptly released her, her dark eyes were as large and as liquid as a startled doe's and several strands of ebony silk had escaped in a riot of soft tendrils from her pony-tail.

Catching her hand, Leandro calculatingly employed his most devastating smile.

'It is just one night. Isabella…*one* night. We can sleep together in a comfortable bed and really get to know each other. Tomorrow night you will be in a different place again, in a different bed—perhaps in one of the *refugios* where there is scant comfort—and you will think of me and perhaps wonder what it might have been like between us had you agreed to come with me tonight. Life is too short for regrets—do you not agree?'

Isabella's heart nearly stopped beating at the look that came her way from his seductive grey eyes. Her feet still hadn't touched the ground since his almost savagely passionate kiss and the pure devastation it had wrought inside her. No man had ever kissed her with such barely controlled desire… And suddenly Isabella knew that she didn't want Leandro Reyes to be her one big regret. She wanted to look back in years to come and think how fortunate she was that fate had decreed that their paths should cross. She might never experience such burning passion with anyone ever again after this and the irresistible connection she had with Leandro would have to sustain her for the rest of her life if that turned out to be the case... Slipping the strap of her canvas bag awkwardly over her shoulder, she acknowledged his too seductive remark with a hot flurry of excitement and trepidation inside her breast. Her legs were shaking as she spoke.

'I agree that life is too short for regrets. But I want you to know that if I go with you, this isn't the kind of thing I make a habit of doing.'

'Of course.' His eyes danced with disturbing amusement. 'Let me call my friend and arrange for a car to pick us up, then I will pay Señor Varez for our meal and we will go.'

Leandro had left her alone to settle into their room. He was downstairs talking to his friend Benito, who had welcomed Isabella with indisputable warmth yet had still maintained a respectful distance. She had quaked inside when she'd seen where Leandro had brought her. Looming out of the rainy night, the hotel resembled an imposing fortress belonging to the Conquistadors. Now, trying to absorb every feature and facet of the seriously opulent room they'd been given, Isabella glanced down at her rain-splattered shirt and jeans and knew she probably looked a million miles away from the kind of prosperous and well-heeled guests that must stay here.

But, shoring up her sudden anxiety about her appearance, she reminded herself that Leandro obviously felt right at home in his own similar clothing and did not give the slightest indication that he was concerned he might be underdressed. Isabella released her breath on a long, low whistle. By all rights she should be dropping with tiredness after her day's hike, but instead she seemed to be infused with a thrumming restless energy that didn't show any sign of dissipating. As she had mounted the wide curved staircase that led to their room, in the wake of a smiling chambermaid, her legs had been distinctly shaky. The prospect of sleeping with Leandro was dominating all her senses and part of her felt like running away because the reality of that event seemed just too overwhelming to be borne.

He had promised her that he would join her 'very soon' after he had spent a little time with his friend and Isabella's tummy had been performing dizzying cartwheels ever since. Now, glancing around the breathtaking and spacious room with its burnt ochre walls, arched stone windows and stately four-poster bed with its luxurious gold satin counterpane, she desperately strove to stay calm.

She was fighting a losing battle. Isabella had just agreed to spend the night with a highly charismatic, good-looking Spanish film director and it was a quite unbelievable event that could not be treated with anything less than extreme trepidation. Since she'd broken up with Patrick three months ago, she hadn't even dated another man—let alone agreed to spend the night! Dammit! She had a perfect right to be nervous! There was no way she could have anticipated such a disturbing possibility as this to occur.

After calling off her wedding, she'd vowed to herself that from now on she would be concentrating on fulfilling her dream of being a writer—not searching for the *grande passion* that had so far eluded her in life. That could come later, she'd promised herself…*if* she was lucky. And if not—then there would be other passions equally enthralling. She had always wanted to live an extraordinary life, and going out on a limb against all her family's advice to write a book and travel to Northern Spain to research it and walk the Camino was just the start. But now, with the prospect of Leandro knocking at the door at any moment, life was quickly going from extraordinary to just plain unbelievable!

Throwing her bag onto the luxurious bed, Isabella hurried into the bathroom to freshen up. A myriad divine scents assailed her as she entered and she saw that everything a discerning guest could possibly require had been provided in abundance. Crossing to the large porcelain basin complete with gold taps, she splashed some cool water on her face and patted it dry with the pristine white hand towel that hung on a large gold ring beside it. Pulling her rain-dampened hair free from its band, she shook it out over her shoulders as she stared at her reflection in the ornate oval mirror. Her glance settled upon the two bright spots of colour glowing on her cheeks and she voiced her impatience out loud. She *hated* it that she blushed so easily! A shy virginal schoolgirl could probably muster up more composure than Isabella could right now!

God only knew what Emilia would think of the whole affair… But even as she entertained the unwanted thought, Isabella knew with certainty that she wouldn't be revealing the fact that she'd met Leandro Reyes to her sister. Duplicity wasn't in her nature, but this was one occasion when she would not be in a hurry to relate the true facts to anyone. And that meant that Emilia would have to go without her information on the Spanish film director—because it definitely wasn't going to be forthcoming from Isabella.

She squared it with her conscience by reminding herself that Leandro had specifically got her to promise that she would not relate any details of their meeting for her sister to print in her magazine and all he had talked about was the Camino anyway, and *not* himself. She was certain that would be of little interest to someone like Emilia, whose meat and drink relied more on any juicy titbits she could find out about a celebrity's personal life rather than their interest in more esoteric subjects. In fact, when Isabella had told her sister that she was going to Spain to research a book on the Santiago de Compostela, Emilia had professed never even to have *heard* of it.

The sudden knock on the door made her feel quite sickeningly faint. Quickly tidying her dishevelled, damp hair, Isabella stole one final unsatisfactory glance in the mirror before hurrying into the other room to open the door. She hadn't even had the chance to reapply her make-up. Oh, well…he would just have to accept her as he found her. His hands either side of his lean, jean-clad hips, Leandro's too engaging smile was akin to the first sigh-inducing lap of hot water in a scented bath, spilling over fatigued and tense limbs after a long day's work…

a pleasure—up until now—virtually unmatched. That pleasure became even more stunningly entrapping when Isabella met his eyes. It was as though his gaze had fired a honey-tipped arrow straight into her breast and now that honey was seeping slowly and inexorably into her blood. She had the strange sensation of having just revealed *everything* to this disturbing man. Burning heat throbbed through her in a debilitating wave.

'Hi.' Her hands fell to her sides to clutch the edges of her shirt—as if she needed something to hold onto to help ground her increasing sense of unreality.

'My friend Benito tells me that I look like a gypsy you must have found on the road to Santiago. He thinks I have bewitched the nice English girl. What do *you* think, Isabella?'

'What do I think?' Her heart pounded as she surveyed the lazy, contemplative smile that Leandro flicked over her chest before returning in an equally leisurely fashion to her heated face. 'I think that your friend has a fine imagination…that's what I think.' Gypsy, pirate, master storyteller… Leandro Reyes was all those things and more, Isabella thought helplessly.

'And how about your own imagination, Isabella? How does that work for you?'

Leandro saw the hot colour seep into her face even before he had finished speaking. The woman found it almost impossible to disguise her feelings and right now he was fiercely glad to know that Isabella's feelings were very much in concordance with his own as far as their fledgling relationship went. He wanted to take her to bed right now…he could barely wait. All the time he had been talking with Benito, all Leandro had really been able to think about was the sweet señorita who was waiting for him upstairs. If she had turned him away tonight he would have been fiercely disappointed and frustrated and it would not have been an easy task to easily put her rejection aside. The realisation merely added to the intense desirous heat that was already gripping him.

'So?' He shrugged with pretended nonchalance. 'I will come inside so that we can discuss the subject further.'

Isabella stood to one side as he passed her. Then she closed the door and watched his tall figure saunter across to the bed and sit down.

CHAPTER THREE

'So…YOU like it here? Benito is very proud of this place.'

'It's beautiful. I didn't expect anything quite like this,' Isabella admitted nervously, glancing round her.

'He told me to tell you that you enhance it with your own beauty.' Leandro took her breath away with a raffish grin. 'But now you must tell me why you are walking the Santiago de Compostela.' Leaning back on his elbows, he regarded her with nonchalant ease…as if he had relaxation down to an art form. It made Isabella ultra sensitive about her own state of discord with her body. She felt jumpy and apprehensive around him, as if she were contemplating touching burning blue flame. With one penetrating glance, she somehow got the notion that he intuited the very *heart* of her feelings and she had to admit that unsettled her perhaps more than anything. She shivered. Outside, as if to echo the mounting agitation inside her, the rain lashed loudly at the thickly paned windows as though threatening to come inside. Curling a still damp strand of ebony hair round her fingers, Isabella sent up a silent plea for guidance. Never had she needed it more!

'I told you…I'm writing a book on why people

choose to walk it. My grandfather was quite a devout Catholic and he talked about it so much that I—'

'Most pilgrims do not walk the Santiago de Compostela for religious reasons—as I am sure you have already found out, Isabella.' Leandro's devastating smile contained just the tiniest hint of mockery and she knew at that moment that he intuited much more about her than she was comfortable with. Those clear grey eyes of his would be ruthless in discerning the truth. Her thoughts would be as transparent to him as though he looked upon a still, unrippled lake, right down to the bottom.

'I needed some inspiration…as well as a new challenge.'

Finally, deciding to express herself without her guard up for once, Isabella let go of her damp tendril of hair and walked across to the window, carefully bypassing the bed on which Leandro had arranged his disturbingly masculine body with such breathtaking ease on top of the gold satin counterpane. 'I mean, I love my job at the library, but for some reason I started to feel a bit dissatisfied. I suppose I got stuck in a rut. Actually, the sameness of it made me want to scream sometimes! Some people thrive on routine, but I realise I don't. Life shouldn't just be a predictable drudge. There should be some adventure, don't you think?' She shrugged as the strength of her feelings took impassioned hold and she glanced back at the window in a bid to compose herself. 'Anyway…I wasn't totally sure what I wanted to do to make things better, but one of the things I *did* know was that I wanted to write this book. The idea had been there for a long time but frankly I kept talking myself out of it. I thought—I thought people would think I was over-reaching myself in some way…you know? Trying to be too clever.' For 'people' read her family and Patrick. 'I had to make some tough decisions. I broke up with my fiancé and cancelled our wedding. I wasn't being callous… It would never have worked anyway and I thought if I don't do this now—the pilgrimage *and* the book—then I may never again have either the courage or the chance. So here I am. I think I'm walking the Camino to find some courage and inspiration to live a different sort of life…to discover who I *really* am and what I'm capable of… Do you know what I mean?'

Hearing the self-conscious edge to her voice, Leandro silently applauded her honesty. Such a candid response to his question was quite refreshing when he considered the duplicity of some other women he'd been with. She must have felt very strongly about her need for change to call off her wedding. Considering the highly desirable qualities this woman possessed, as well as her enchanting looks, Leandro concluded that her ex-fiancé must have suffered considerable regret about losing her. Isabella Deluce was a fascinating, indisputably *sexy* woman, who *any* man could not fail to be affected by. Uncoiling his body from the bed, he strolled casually across to the window to join her.

'Isabella…'

Examining the rippling silk that was her rich dark hair, he gently parted some strands with his fingers and softly blew his warm breath onto the back of her neck. He saw her exquisitely sensitive shiver and was fiercely glad that he had brought her here to Benito's luxurious hotel in the middle of the night where there was little possibility that any paparazzi would be following him. If they did... Benito knew exactly what to do to get rid of them. Now all Leandro aimed to do was to devote himself to Isabella for the whole of the rest of the night *without* interruption. 'Every footstep you take on the Camino is taking you back to yourself...your *true* self,' he told her. 'I promise you that. By the time you reach the Cathedral in Santiago at the end of your walking and pass through the famous Door of Glory as millions of pilgrims have done before you, you will have much more clarity of mind and heart.'

Instinctively Isabella knew that Leandro was right and his words definitely raised her spirits. Already, after days and miles of walking, sometimes in silence, sometimes with the companionship of other walkers, and at night as bands of them joined together in various villages dotted across Northern Spain for the nightly pilgrims' mass, Isabella knew a deeply profound change was taking place inside her. As Leandro had said, most people did *not* walk the Camino for religious reasons. Undertaking the challenging five-hundred-mile trek on foot walking through vineyards and the ancient kingdoms of Northern Spain in the hot sun, wind and rain certainly gave a person plenty of time to reflect.

Already Isabella knew it would impact upon her life for ever and she hadn't even completed it yet. But she'd already discovered on the way that there was so much more to Isabella Deluce than just being a dutiful daughter and a good librarian. She had cut loose from a fiancé who secretly mocked the true meaning of love and was bereft of any feeling of loyalty towards her whatsoever, and had also turned her back on the advice of a family who saw only pitfalls ahead in making the decisions she had. Isabella had relinquished these things to find herself in a part of Spain that was so far away from the frantic tourism of the Costas that it was almost like another country entirely. A part of the country that endured disparate extremes of weather—the rain pounding down on the red clay of the mesas one minute and the baking sun turning the earth into a veritable oven in the next. It couldn't fail to arouse a sense of wonder and mystery in the soul of anyone who surrendered to its magic.

If that wasn't enough, now with Leandro she found herself surrendering to magic of a different kind... His teasing breath feathering the back of her neck was a sweet melting heat that rippled over Isabella's senses like a sensual summer breeze. Leandro Reyes was blessed with the kind of sizzling sexual allure that would induce a clarion call of longing in any woman whose gaze happened to collide with his. Even the air around him seemed to be charged with his deeply affecting presence.

'You smell of the wild flowers in the mountains.'

'Do I?'

She turned round to gaze into his fascinating silver-grey eyes, feeling his melting glance bathe her in sensuous moonlight. His lashes were astonishingly luxurious considering they belonged to a man so masculine, and with startling realisation Isabella silently and nervously acknowledged the burning haze of desire that was shockingly directed towards her. 'I've spent days and days walking in nature.' She offered him a wry smile. 'Maybe some of it's rubbed off on me?'

Her smile slowly dissipated in the disquieting absence of his reply. Instead, her body silently shook with the need for him to touch her. Isabella knew his taste now and because she knew it, she *craved* it. In that moment it was hard to envisage anything that would excite and please her more. She was getting used to expecting the miraculous on this journey; the heavens answered her prayer. She'd hardly taken her next breath when Leandro started to run his hands slowly down the outside of her arms, bringing her trembling form into disturbingly close contact with his own. '*You* are one of nature's exquisite mysteries too, Isabella. You remind me of the most rare of beautiful wild flowers…of the delight of spring after a long, harsh winter. And you stir in me a heat so powerful, it is like the burning sun that scorches the mesas…'

'I do?' Her voice descended to a whisper.

'*Sí*…you do. I want to seduce you, Isabella…very much…and I have waited too long already.'

Bending his dark head towards her, Leandro touched his mouth to hers. Isabella's startled gasp was swept away on a blissful wave of unutterable delight as he kissed her. His lips tasted faintly of Albarino wine and dark Brazilian coffee, and right then she could not have envisaged a more arousing combination of flavours— deliciously heightened by the unmatchable essence of the man himself. The ravishingly hot sweep of his tongue was a sensation she wanted to revisit again and again and again… There would never be such a thing as 'too much' where Leandro was concerned.

Unable to restrain her own need, Isabella groaned hungrily into his mouth as he cupped the back of her head to bring her closer still and followed the curve of her spine with his free hand, straight down to her bottom. Squeezing and kneading her flesh, Leandro provocatively aligned her hips with his own, then moved them teasingly apart again—repeating the action with even more deliberate and devastating precision until Isabella seriously feared for her sanity if he were to continue with such a sexy little game for much longer. She wanted him inside her...her body demanded it. Even as the thought made her cheeks burn, her hips had seemingly softened in preparation for his lovemaking. Her breasts had grown heavy and she felt shivery and *weak* all over—a completely intense reaction that was quite unlike anything she'd ever experienced with any other man before.

There was the devil's own smile on Leandro's mesmerising face as his lips broke contact with hers and Isabella left her hands either side of his taut lean middle so that she wouldn't lose her balance, because there was a real danger that she would. Words deserted her but she held his melting, knowing smile with a steady answering gaze even as her heart quietly pounded.

'I want to make love to you all night... Do you know that? Even then, I seriously doubt whether that will satisfy my need to possess you!' Threading his fingers through her hair, Leandro focused on her with laser-like concentration.

Overwhelmed by his attention, Isabella clamped her

teeth down self-consciously on her lip. Her heart was now beating with hypnotic rhythm inside her chest. 'By rights I should really be getting some rest,' she told him breathlessly, suddenly terrified by the virtual forest fire of lust they had ignited between them. 'I—I have another long walk ahead of me tomorrow.'

'We will make love...*then* we will rest.'

Possessively clasping her hand, Leandro commandingly steered Isabella over to the bed. He sank down onto it pulling her onto his lap. His hands were warm and hard and she sensed the urgency in them. The only other sound in the room was the gentle creak of the mattress and the now less violent hiss of the rain as it hit the windows. As Leandro studied her face her gaze held his with a silent devastating plea, and the deep river of lust that was compelling him to be with this woman flowed with even more forceful demand in his veins. Had he ever witnessed such palpable longing in a woman's eyes before?

As he tipped up Isabella's chin the edges of Leandro's lips lifted a little in a deeply satisfied smile. Her brow was so smooth and fair with little obvious hint that she'd been walking in strong sunshine for days now and her compelling eyes were as dark as the black robes of a nun.

Running his glance across her sexy mouth, he saw that her lips still carried the faint trace of moisture from his and as he observed them with increasingly ravenous thirst he witnessed just the tiniest quiver. If she were an actress and he were directing her in a love scene, he would be instructing the most heart-stopping close-up of her features right now and her lovely face would stay in the mind long after the closing credits had rolled.

Heady desire sweeping through him like a fierce tornado, the buttons on Isabella's shirt irresistibly beckoned and Leandro obeyed the deep, silent, fevered impulse to undo them. A trickle of sweat sluggishly meandered down the middle of his back and clung to his heated skin as he did so. The heat in the room was bordering on sultry and weighed on the air like a heavy overcoat but he knew too that later on tonight it would be a different story. In early May, as it was now, the mornings could be piercingly chill to the point of ice, but by midday the sun would be roasting, burning down on the landscape in a relentless haze. More compelling to Leandro, however, was the fever of carnal need that had taken his body prisoner. His mind became emptied of every thought but *Isabella*, conjuring up rich, erotic fantasies of what they would do together, his strong abdominal muscles bunching hard to constrain his rapidly escalating desire. He should not overwhelm her...this enchanting English girl who was walking the Santiago de Compostela trail to 'find' herself. He had no wish to be the one discordant note in her symphony of self-discovery. Yet Leandro would not deny himself this exquisite opportunity to discover her in the most intimate way. He wanted her far too much for that and so he would take what he wanted without regret.

Isabella gasped when Leandro's lean, bronzed hands practically tore open her blouse and pushed it down over her shoulders. Her full breasts bounced a little in her white balconette bra and she felt her nipples pinch tight. When she dared a greedy glance at the beautifully hewn masculine features and light copper skin that was so close to her, she immediately ached with almost violent need. Nothing could adequately convey this man's stunning allure, she was certain—but Isabella knew her memory would not fail her. Now his hungry stare grazed lasciviously on her breasts and she ached for the sweet release of his hot mouth caressing them, unconsciously pursing her lips to moisten them a little at the flagrantly erotic thought.

Then he kissed her, splaying his palm against the back of her head to hold her fast, and it barely took even a second for Isabella to pay him back with the hot, hungry response his lips almost brutally demanded. The explosion between them was a nuclear fusion of white hot heat. Already Leandro's sizzling X-rated kisses had ruined Isabella for life. Withdrawing from her with a teasing little smile, he practically ripped open the buttons of his shirt to reveal a chest so beautifully defined with lean, hard muscle that Isabella sucked in her breath and let it out slowly again, in awe. After that, she couldn't have said who undressed whom, all she knew was that taking their clothes off had become an imperative tide that they could not turn back from, and as hands grasped and mouths clashed Isabella likened the furore of sensation soaring through her blood to a fire ripping through a dry forest...a fire that could not be doused with even a *lake* of water.

With passionately voiced whispers of appreciation and encouragement, Leandro caressed her hips, her breasts, her thighs, his deliciously erotic hands elevating the tension between them with every stroke, heatedly encouraging Isabella's growing desire to break all its previously guarded bounds and simply surrender. Her nervousness dissipated like a snowflake in the sun as she relinquished her natural inhibition, and discovered a spontaneous lustful side to her character instead. A quality that frankly was a revelation to her. And she no longer had to hope or wish or *yearn* to have the attentions of Leandro's mouth on her breasts—not when he was in turn taking her exquisitely tight nipples deep into the moist cavern of his mouth and driving her near mad with the need to have him inside her. His body was a mouth-watering study in masculine perfection too. Lean but muscular—every perfectly delineated, smooth-as-silk muscle in that copper skinned torso was a fascinating revelation never to be forgotten.

Briefly thinking about the promised phone-call to her sister, Isabella knew she'd already abandoned the idea. If Emilia even *guessed* that her 'principled' big sister had wound up in bed with a man she'd only just met and that man happened to be the very man she'd dispatched Isabella to try and win an interview with for her magazine…then Isabella would never hear the end of it! But once she started back on the Camino trail tomorrow, no one would be able to contact her, thank God. She would once again know some peace from her demanding family.

'Isabella…' Leandro's hot breath skimmed erotically over the delicate skin on her ear '…*usted es tan hermoso, asi que fino.*' She recognised the Spanish for 'beautiful' and 'fine' and shivered with pleasure.

* * *

A woman's scent had always been the biggest turn-on for Leandro, but surely Isabella's had the undeniable power to drive a man 'loco' with desire? He decided this because he wanted her with an almost feral lustfulness that left him breathless and aching as he had never ached for a woman before. His body was all but crying out for him to make that final inevitable connection with hers and it was strange—but he almost intuited a sense of destiny as he stroked his hands over her temptingly curvy hips and slid his muscular, more hirsute legs down over hers. Quickly dismissing the unsettling thought, he told himself that sexual desire could stir the most outrageously fanciful ideas in a man and he should be careful. Isabella was a beguiling woman, that was true, but at the end of the day all Leandro wanted to do was enjoy her beautiful body for a while...not *marry* her! When his fingers slid over the scalding heat of her womanhood, then inside her provocative wetness, he heard her sharp, excited intake of breath and momentarily lost himself in the stunning eroticism of the highly charged moment. The sensation almost unravelled him right there. At her small ecstatic moan, he smiled, kissed her softly on the mouth, then raised himself up from her trembling form and leaned across the bed to reach for his jeans. Taking out his wallet from the back pocket, he withdrew one of two foil-wrapped condoms that had been concealed in the zipped compartment and, sitting back, carefully sheathed himself with it. When he returned to Isabella, his knee urged her trembling legs apart—his expression a deeply masculine study in unleashed passion as he did so—and gratifyingly sensed her clasp his body tightly with her slender silken thighs. Then, slowly and with almost agonising pleasure, Leandro eased his hard, aching shaft deep inside her. *Madre mia!* She was fire and satin, this exquisite woman, and her expressive dark eyes locked sensually onto his as he started to ride her.

Her eyes drifted closed as the growing sensual tension inside her inexorably built with each demanding thrust into her body. They swiftly opened again in shock as Leandro said fiercely, 'Look at me, Isabella! Do not hide your pleasure from me! I want to witness everything!' As the tension reached an exquisite plateau and sensual waves ebbed through her with force Isabella's heartbeat went wild. In those highly charged moments, she knew a deepening sense of destiny. For whatever reason fate decreed...she had been meant to meet Leandro Reyes...even if it *was* just for this one night. A harsh, soul-deep cry left his lips just then and punctured the sultry air—the surprising sound resonating with force in the room and momentarily silencing the sound of the rain as his body quivered hard with release. Isabella was enthralled by that uninhibited shout of pleasure and for long moments she just allowed herself to simply bask in her woman's power. The idea was a new and exciting revelation to add to her already growing store of new discoveries.

Curling her hands round Leandro's sleek, hard biceps, she felt her heart hammer inside her chest almost as heavily and as fast as the relentless rain that pummelled the window-panes. Then she moved her fingers through his mane of thick dark hair, secretly loving the sensation of his muscular body covering hers, pressing her down deep into the mattress—the erotic sheen of his sweat glazing her skin and her senses filled with the scent of their lovemaking.

'You have confirmed my suspicions quite emphatically, Isabella. Rest will be the furthest thing from my mind now that my body has known the deep, deep pleasure of joining with yours.'

Along with this wry, hungry observation, Leandro accorded Isabella with the most dangerously challenging smile she'd ever received. If that seriously fever-inducing gesture wasn't enough, the look in his clear grey eyes literally made her heart leap. 'Instead we will make love and listen to the rain and make love again until we are close to exhaustion, my sweet Isabella,' he asserted.

His deliberately possessive 'my' resonating with undeniable delight throughout her entire being, Isabella sensed renewed desire swiftly build inside her even as Leandro bent his head and his lips hungrily claimed a breast. She slowly released a softly ragged breath, the ache between her legs almost painful. 'I want that too,' she whispered, without any trace of doubt or inhibition…

The arrival of the morning sneaked into her consciousness far too soon. Awake as soon the sky started to lighten in the east, spreading the pink tinge of dawn across the previously black canvas of the night, Isabella breathed out softly as she studied the arresting sleeping features of Leandro beside her. Although clearly surrendering to fatigue now, they'd paid scant attention to sleep during the past few hours. As she felt her face suffuse with warmth as she recalled how emphatically she and her Spanish lover had whiled those precious night-time hours away the corners of Isabella's lush mouth couldn't help but edge upwards into a smile. This morning she was a different woman *again* from the one that had been slowly emerging during the pilgrimage. She'd already been feeling braver and stronger but now after last night...she felt *daring* too. And her body brimmed with a new vitality even though she ached in every muscle...her tender spots arising because of the amazing man lying beside her.

Isabella might well smile. Just then Leandro stirred, rubbed a hand round his beard-roughened chiselled jaw and opened his eyes. It was like staring right into a pool of silvery starlight... Isabella's stomach dived straight to her feet in stunning awareness of the shock of that direct arresting gaze.

'*Buenos días.*'

Before she could even reply, Leandro slid his fingers beneath her chin and claimed her mouth in a deeply sat-isfying—and bordering on ravenous—kiss.

'Good morning,' she croaked, her black-coffee eyes wide with surprise and pleasure.

As Leandro lazily surveyed Isabella's early-morning face, her bewitching beauty undimmed by lack of rest, her long dark hair spilling over her smooth bare shoul-ders and her tentative smile intriguingly self-conscious, his stomach clutched with surprising regret at the thought of having to say goodbye to her today. This woman had given him such stunning and unforgettable pleasure—both with her body *and* her company and he was not quite ready to relinquish either. Leandro found himself wishing that they could spend the rest of the day in bed and let the world carry on without them. But inevitably they *must* part—he to return to his house to catch up with some urgent reading of new manuscripts and work proposals before returning to Madrid to embark upon his latest cinematic project—and she to continue this most ancient of pilgrimages, presumably followed by her own return to her homeland...

'I could wish to be woken in such a satisfying way *every* morning, my fair Isabella.' There it was again...that very appealing and possessive 'my'. Used in such a seductive way, the huskily voiced note of ownership could not possibly offend her...*quite the opposite*. Allowing him to pull her against his chest and smooth back her tousled dark fringe from her face, Isabella breathed in Leandro's addictive soft musk scent as he grinned at her suggestively.

She had to attempt at least twenty miles today through varying and challenging terrain if she was to catch up with some walking companions as arranged and the memory of that wicked and gorgeous smile of his was surely going to sustain her until she reached the monastery where she had planned to stay tonight... But at the thought of parting from Leandro, Isabella felt a hollow little flutter inside her chest and then the same again—only stronger—in the pit of her stomach.

'You've hardly had any sleep at all and now I've woken you,' she said apologetically.

'And I was the very inconsiderate man who kept you awake most of the night because I could not keep my hands off of you! You should not be endowed with so many beguiling qualities to tempt me so much!' He laughed huskily. Isabella wanted to say, I'll miss you, but then she remembered that Leandro Reyes was a very well known and respected film director and once he had returned to his busy and demanding life her memory would be relegated very firmly to his past. She knew she wasn't special. Working in the film industry as he did, he would have every opportunity to bed the most alluring women and probably *did*. She would be just one of *many*. Her stomach protested with a sickening twist at the thought…

'I should get up and get dressed,' she murmured, deliberately averting her gaze away from the cynosure of his piercing silvery eyes…the eyes that seemed to see into her soul. She'd best just start to forget him right now if that were possible and focus on the pilgrimage instead. 'I've got to get back to my hotel and get some breakfast and fill my water bottle before I get going again.'

'Benito's driver will drop us both back when we are ready,' Leandro responded immediately, 'but we can breakfast here first.'

'I'd rather not, if you don't mind? I have to make up quite a bit of time today.' Moving away from him, she sat up, using some of the sheet to hide her nakedness. For some reason, a strong wave of protectiveness for the vulnerability the gesture exposed washed over Leandro.

Once again he had cause to admonish himself for his un-characteristic reaction. Isabella and he had had a good time in bed…an *unbelievable* time, in fact…but at the end of the day she was just another beautiful girl passing through and in a few days' time, when she had com-pleted the pilgrimage, she would be going home again to England. End of story… So long as she did not relate any of what had occurred between them to her sister or anyone else associated with the media, Leandro would relegate their time together to a very pleasurable and warm memory.

'So?' He sat up too, the warm skin on his thigh brushing up against hers. He sensed her answering shiver and felt a strong leap of desire. He quelled it. 'When you go back to England…where is home?' he asked casually.

A quizzical little crease appeared between Isabella's fine dark brows, as though she was surprised he should ask such a question.

'I live in Islington in London…the least posh part. Do you know it?'

'I have heard of it.' Leandro smiled. 'And you work nearby?'

'In Highgate. It's not far away.'

'And you will be busy working on your book when you return, *sí*?'

Isabella shrugged self-consciously, the movement dislodging the sheet and suddenly exposing her bare breasts. She quickly grabbed it back again and covered herself. 'That's the plan. And you…you'll be working on a film I guess?'

Immediately the shutters came down over Leandro's

eyes and Isabella could have kicked herself. She'd hate to think that he might believe she would tell anybody anything that he'd told her...*especially* about his work or his private life. Considering that both were topics he'd deliberately avoided discussing during their time together, he must know he had nothing to fear?

'I will be getting back to work, *sí*. Isabella?'

'Yes?' Her dark eyes widened as she watched his hand scrape through his tousled hair.

'I would give you my phone number but it is not something that I do readily or easily. In my position, I have to be careful...you understand?' His words confirmed she was not important to him in any way as well as reiterating his intense need to guard his privacy. Fielding the immense wave of hurt and disappointment that washed over her, Isabella briefly inclined her head. 'Yes, I understand.'

'Why don't you use the shower first?' he suggested smoothly and she could easily sense his withdrawal from her. 'I have a couple of phone calls to make before we leave.'

'Okay.' She felt as if she'd been somehow dismissed from his life as though she were nothing but an afterthought, and Isabella's heart was sickeningly heavy as she turned her back to get out of bed...

CHAPTER FOUR

Eighteen Months Later... London, England.

'I'M SORRY I'm back a little late, Natasha, but Chris and I went for coffee after the film. Is Raphael asleep?'

'He's sound as anything. I don't even think an earthquake would wake him! And you're not late at all...I told you not to rush. You could have gone for a meal or something instead of just a coffee. How was it?'

The petite blonde stood back from the door to allow Isabella entry, watching her friend unbutton her long black coat, then unwind her cerise knitted scarf and hang them both on the pine-wood coat-stand inside the hall.

'How was what?' she asked distractedly, blowing briefly down onto her chilled hands. The November weather was icy tonight, with the wind as lethal as a sharpened razor. The past few winters had been almost strangely mild but this one was kicking in with a vengeance, it seemed. Northern Spain and those sun-drenched mesas seemed a million miles away.

Mockingly lifting her pale, perfectly shaped brows,

Natasha put her hands on her almost stick-thin hips. 'The *film*, of course! What did you think I meant?'

Isabella almost didn't want to discuss the film. Instead she wanted to stow the memory of it away and savour the details later when she was alone—like a treat she wanted to keep for herself and didn't want to share. The story had touched her deeply. It had been about a mother's relationship with her son...a son who, when he was grown, had rejected his simple country background in every sense because he had been so thoroughly seduced by the apparent 'glamour' of western culture. So seduced that he'd turned his back even on the woman who'd raised him. The director had been one *Leandro Reyes*. Even if Isabella had never had the good fortune to meet the man, she would have instantly been a fan after seeing this movie. It had been done exquisitely sensitively and, although emotions had unquestioningly been stirred, never at any time had Leandro's sublime direction allowed the audience to be manipulated by them. He'd simply let the story and the consummate skill of the actors playing the parts speak for themselves—yet the guiding hand he'd wielded was unmistakable. Leaving the cinema afterwards with her friend Chris, Isabella had been in silent awe at what she'd witnessed.

'The film was wonderful! You should try and get to see it some time. I couldn't recommend it highly enough.'

Both women turned automatically towards the kitchen. Isabella because she was in dire need of a soothing cup of chamomile tea to calm emotions that had been charged quite unremittingly by Leandro's film, and

Natasha because she was eager to hear any titbits of gossip that Isabella and Chris had shared in her absence.

'You know me. I don't really go for those intellectual art-house films. Give me a nice uncomplicated romantic comedy any day!'

'But it wasn't trying to be intellectual at all.'

Reaching the kitchen, Isabella filled the electric kettle with water, then plugged it in at the socket next to the toaster. Opening an overhead cupboard, she retrieved a chamomile teabag and dropped it into her favourite patterned pottery mug. 'Tea or coffee?' she asked her friend.

'Neither, thanks. I had a coffee just before you got back and I really should go home, to be honest. I've got to be up early to open the nursery at eight.'

'Okay…but like I was saying…' Isabella folded her arms across the black ribbed sweater she wore with her red corduroy skirt, a slight frown between her dark brows '…the film wasn't coming from the intellect at all… It was coming from the heart.'

Shrugging a little self-consciously because she knew that she'd expressed her opinion so passionately, Isabella tried to fend off her natural fear that she shouldn't reveal her feelings quite so vociferously. Keeping her deeper emotions mostly hidden was something she had learned by necessity to do so that she wouldn't make waves with her family. And even though she did buck the trend every now and then—such as when she'd called off her wedding to Patrick and upset *everybody*—somehow the trait had translated to other relationships too. And sometimes, Isabella reflected, the insights and revelations she had learned on the Camino were not always ready to be shared with others…

Generally, people didn't like you raising topics that made them question the purpose of their own lives. Most folk got along quite happily pretending that everything was fine, she had found—even when it clearly wasn't.

'Anyway—' Natasha grinned '—how's Chris getting on with this new bloke of hers? Do you think he'll last beyond two or three dates as is her usual record?'

Chris had confided in Isabella that she really liked this new man she was seeing and, yes, she definitely *did* have hopes that the relationship would last beyond her usual quota of a couple of dates. Her friend yearned to get married and start a family and, at thirty-one years old, had started to fear that it might never happen. Tonight she had confessed to Isabella that she envied her being the mother of a baby son…

At the thought of her little boy, a bubble of joy seemed to burst inside her and Isabella happily antici-pated cuddling him later and reacquainting herself with that most delicious of baby scents at the back of his adorable neck. She couldn't deny she was looking forward to her favourite occupation—spending precious time with her beautiful child. He had truly become the centre of her whole world. For her, walking the Camino Way back in the spring of last year had been even more life changing than she'd anticipated. Now she had Raphael…the unexpected 'gift' she'd received from her incredible night of passion with Leandro Reyes. The discovery that she was pregnant had honestly come as the most stupendous of shocks.

They'd been so careful, she'd recalled hotly, even as a stomach-rolling memory had disturbingly nudged her recall—of being half asleep in the dead of night with the shrill repetitive drone of cicadas filling the hot, sultry air and hearing Leandro murmur as if dreaming... Isabella...my Isabella...' before reaching out to her... Raphael had been conceived during those somehow 'unreal' moments when they'd both thought they were dreaming, and Isabella's previous life, as a young single woman who'd been feeling vaguely dissatisfied and in turmoil about her future and who had chosen to walk the path of an ancient pilgrimage to 'find' herself, had been changed for ever. Now, forcing her attention back to the present and a quizzical-looking Natasha, who was clearly wondering what Isabella was looking so 'dreamy' about, she flushed a little guiltily. 'I think that you should talk to Chris herself about that.' She smiled and turned to fill her mug with the hot water that had boiled.

'Trying to get some gossip out of you is like trying to get a politician to tell the truth! Bloody impossible! What amazes me is that you and your sister couldn't be more different! Emilia wouldn't hesitate to ditch any principles for a juicy story or a job promotion, yet you have enough for the whole of the UK!'

Stirring her tea and extracting the squeezed teabag, Isabella laid it carefully on a saucer and turned back to calmly regard her exasperated friend. It was ironic really. Her parents thought she had *no* principles for sleeping with some 'opportunist stranger' she'd met in Spain and getting pregnant by him and yet her friends thought she was too principled for words! She couldn't win. 'I'm honestly not trying to be holier than thou or anything; I just think it's Chris's business, that's all. As for my sister—' she frowned '—I want to be able to sleep tonight so I don't think I'll open that particular can of worms if you don't mind!'

The relationship between the two women was even more strained than usual. Emilia had been frosty with Isabella ever since she'd returned from Spain last year and had not produced the demanded 'interview' with Leandro Reyes as she'd hoped—but Isabella had already decided that she was not going to divulge anything about her meeting with the renowned film director to anybody. Their time together had been so precious, so amazing, that she didn't want to sully the memory of it with gossip. When she'd discovered that she was pregnant by Leandro, she'd strengthened that personal vow even more. Not even Isabella's parents knew who her little son's father was... And even though they clearly doted on their unexpected grandchild, they'd declared them-selves to be 'mortally disappointed' in their eldest daughter for yet again letting down the side.

'Well, if you're not going to spill any beans, then I'm afraid I'm just going to have to love you and leave you.' Her innate good nature overwhelming her disappoint-ment at not learning any new gossip, Natasha stepped towards the dark-haired girl and gave her a genuinely fond hug. 'Honestly, though, I'm happy to look after Raphael any time. He's an absolute angel as well as being utterly gorgeous and you've made all your girlfriends green with envy...dedicated career women or not!'

'Thanks, Natasha. It's been a great help to me to be able to leave him at your nursery when I'm working at the library. I know for sure he's in good hands.'

'You're welcome. And perhaps I'll go see that film you saw tonight at the weekend? See if it's as wonderful as you say it is.'

'You won't be disappointed, I promise you.'

Already the film had become monumentally important to Isabella because it was yet another precious link to the man she'd given her heart to all those months ago…the man who was unknowingly the father of her baby.

Walking her friend to the door and helping her on with her coat, Isabella turned eagerly towards the bedroom as the other woman finally left, unable to wait even one moment longer to see her sleeping child…

Tipping out the contents of his wallet to search for a telephone number he needed, Leandro came upon a small gold business card from his friend Benito's hotel. He hadn't been in touch with him since that night he'd taken Isabella there and now he dropped down into the faded leather chair behind his desk and frowned in deep concentration. All kinds of disturbing emotions seemed to flare in his blood as he continued to broodingly stare at the small embossed card. An avalanche of heat flooded his senses as Leandro recalled that amazing, sexually charged night he'd spent with Isabella. *Isabella…*

Such a longing arose inside him at the memory of the dark-haired English girl he had been so enamoured with that he'd seduced her on the very first night they'd met and for a moment the depth of that longing was a hollow, aching void in the centre of Leandro's chest. He had thought about her often since bidding her goodbye outside her hotel in the Port of Vigo and there had been many a time that he had regretted his cautious decision not to give her his telephone number so that they could stay in touch.

But what was she doing now? He longed to know. Had walking the Santiago de Compostela brought her the clarity and sense of purpose that she had hoped it would? Knowing what he knew, Leandro could not doubt that it had. Perversely, in the months that had followed their parting, his personal sense of purpose had been in turmoil. He had won more acclaim for his work than he had ever dreamed of, with offers coming even from Hollywood to further his directorial career. Yet he had also lost his father just a month after meeting Isabella and the loss had been almost too hard to bear.

Suddenly work was not the exciting prospect that took precedence over everything. He was like a wounded soldier who had forgotten to keep his guard up in battle and had unexpectedly been cut down by a sword or a bayonet. His father's death had been sudden, shocking, his life stolen in one dreadful moment by a drunken driver, and that had made his passing even worse.

Theirs had been a remarkable relationship. As well as being the most amiable and best of men to get along with, Vincente Reyes had been the most dedicated fan of Leandro's film work. Yet Leandro had not been able to fulfil the one wish that his father had longed to see come true before he died. He had wanted to see his only son married and a father and would have liked nothing better than a grandson or daughter to dote on. But Leandro had not had a long-term girlfriend in nearly three years...how could he even *think* about a relationship when basically his life was more or less devoted to his work?

But now as he remembered the intensity of emotion he had experienced that night with Isabella, he seriously thought about getting in touch with her again. Thinking of his father and the brutal realisation that life could be so suddenly and frighteningly snatched away, it had made Leandro increasingly sense the importance of making a connection somewhere with another human being. A much more personal connection than he had made in a long, long time. If Isabella had a relationship or was married, then he would leave well alone. However, if she were not...then what would be the harm in arranging to see her again? Feeling his blood throb with purpose, Leandro reached towards the telephone on his desk, automatically punching out a number he used regularly to make travel reservations...

It had been a long day and her throbbing feet and aching back were testimony to just *how* long a day it had been. She'd practically been standing since she'd come in that morning at nine and now it was just after five in the afternoon. Isabella had never been a 'clock watcher' but when you became a parent, she'd discovered, time took on a whole new meaning. It became infinitely precious. Now she was almost resentful of every second that she spent away from her little boy. Stealing another glance at the clock on the wall behind the long curved counter where she stood, she made a neat stack of the letters that needed to go out tonight on her way home and considered the compelling luxury of a long hot bath to ease her tired, aching limbs after she'd put Raphael to bed.

'Cup of coffee?'

Her fair-haired colleague leaned over the counter, taking Isabella by surprise.

'Becky! You startled me.'

'Daydreaming about that baby of yours again?' Becky grinned. Only just eighteen, the engaging teenager was on a day-release scheme from a local college and quite frankly her unflagging enthusiasm and willingness to learn had been invaluable to the library team. Isabella had grown quite fond of the girl.

'One day you'll know what it's like.' She smiled back, her dark eyes twinkling.

'Not until I'm thirty-five at least! I want to have plenty of fun before I settle down and have a family. Anyway, how about that cup of coffee?'

'That would be great...thanks.'

Isabella was reflecting on what Becky had said, asking herself if she'd relinquish 'having fun' if the choice were presented to her again over having a child, and decided immediately that there was really no contest. Raphael provided all the joy and fun she needed... Smiling to herself at the delicious feeling of warmth that flooded her being at the thought of her little boy's sweet angelic face, Isabella lifted her gaze towards the swing doors of the entrance and the sight she saw there almost made her stop breathing... Leandro!

Was she dreaming? She blinked twice in rapid succession to make sure and was faced with the full, astounding reality of his flesh-and-blood presence. The palms of her hands flattened on the wooden counter needing the support. Even at the distance between them, those fascinating silvery eyes of his burned with a heat that made her feel weak. Wearing a long, fashionable black coat over an equally dark shirt and jeans, with his tousled hair, chiseled jaw and Mediterranean skin he brought an irresistible *dangerous* allure into the sedately benign surroundings of the public library. Isabella sensed her mouth turn dry as chalk as he approached and she knew that hers weren't the only eyes to track his progress. The man was simply *compelling...*

'*Buenos días, Isabella.*'

'How—how did you find me?'

He smiled and Isabella saw a flash of white teeth and a sexy little dimple appear at one corner of his fascinating mouth. 'I was working my way round all the libraries in the area, believe it or not. This is the third one I have tried... How fortunate is that?'

Isabella remembered telling him before they parted that she worked in Highgate. She wondered why he had left it eighteen months before coming to look for her. More than that, *why* had he come at all? Her stomach started to churn as her thoughts naturally turned to her son... *Leandro's son too.*

'I don't understand what you're doing here?' she breathed, her hand unconsciously flattening against her belly, where tumult reigned supreme.

* * *

Isabella was definitely the sexiest librarian that Leandro had ever seen... Being so close to her again after eighteen long months, he felt his blood pound with helpless sensual excitement. It was clear by his extremely positive reaction that he had done the right thing in trying to find her. Now all he craved was the chance to be alone with her. He was impatient that she was here working, when all his instincts yearned to whisk her off somewhere and make love. His hungry gaze leisurely tracked her body in her dark green belted blouse and long black skirt. She was wearing her hair up too and Leandro longed to unpin it and see it cascade down over her shoulders. Anticipatory heat tightened his groin.

'I wanted to see you again, of course.'

'That's a little hard to believe after so long,' she answered defensively, a pink stain spreading on her cheeks.

He shrugged, convinced he could win her round. It might be arrogance on his part, but it was obvious to Leandro that he was definitely having an effect on her.

'When do you finish work? We have to talk.'

'"Have" to?' Her dark eyes flashed her annoyance. 'I don't *have* to do anything that *you* want me to do! You didn't even have the courtesy to give me your phone number when we said goodbye in Spain! Now you turn up as casually as though it were just yesterday we saw each other!' She raised her voice, hissing her anger and people were looking. Isabella's cheeks turned even pinker.

Leandro could not deny his own irritation in response. Perhaps he should not have been so quick to imagine that she would be glad to see him again, but he certainly had not expected to be openly castigated for seeking her out!

'You know full well the reason I did not give you my number! But this is not the time and place for us to have this conversation. That should be in private when we are alone. What time do you finish here?' he asked again, his silvery gaze almost fierce. Isabella sighed heavily and Leandro saw her charged breathing tighten her blouse a little across her breasts. He swallowed hard, watching her collect the little pile of white envelopes on the counter in front of her and hold them to her chest, almost as if to protect herself.

Isabella hardly trusted herself to speak. All she really wanted to do was go somewhere and have a good cry. But weeping would not accomplish anything and even though she'd flared up at Leandro about talking, they definitely *needed* to have a conversation! She had to tell him about his son. It had never been her decision to keep his existence a secret. Leandro was the one who had forced that decision on her by not giving Isabella his telephone number or at least *somewhere* where she might contact him and give him the news. She had longed to share with him that their passionate union that night had created a wonderful little boy, yet at the same time she had also dreaded it because she feared his reaction. If he had dismissed their time together as just another one-night stand, as Isabella was pretty sure Leandro *had*—then the last thing he would want to hear was that he had a son! But now that he had turned up in her life again, Isabella was experiencing confusion as well as anger.

'I finish at five-thirty, but I need to go straight home tonight. If I give you my phone number perhaps we can arrange to meet tomorrow evening?' She was only delaying their talk because she had to go to the nursery first and collect Raphael. That hardly gave her enough time to compose herself and think how she was going to break the astounding news to Leandro that he'd become a father! She saw the dismissive shake of his dark head with trepidation.

'No. I do not want to wait until tomorrow to talk to you! If you need to go home first then I will wait until you finish and we will go back to your house together.'

Isabella had to think *fast*. She could see that Leandro was in no mood to be amenable about this, yet she desperately needed *some* time to get herself together! And she'd frankly rather talk to him first before letting him see Raphael. She wondered if she could prevail upon either Natasha or Chris to baby-sit?

Suddenly noticing Becky make her way past the long line of computers where the public utilised the Internet—the promised cup of coffee clasped between her hands—Isabella glanced pleadingly up into Leandro's forbidding handsome gaze. 'If you could give me a couple of hours to sort myself out, I can go home, do what I have to do, then meet you somewhere where we can talk? Please, Leandro…'

'Why don't you come to me then?' he suggested, a flash of impatience in his eyes at having to wait to see her at all. Drawing an empty white envelope towards him, he wrote down an address. 'A friend of mine has loaned me his house for a few days. We can talk, then go out to dinner.'

'Okay…I'll do that. I'll come to you.'

'Here you are!' Becky put down the steaming beverage in front of Isabella, then glanced sidelong at Leandro. Immediately Isabella saw the interested gleam that stole into her bright blue eyes. She found herself praying that the teenager wouldn't mention anything about Raphael. A public confrontation was the last thing she needed!

'No biscuits, I'm afraid…but then that's probably a blessing. Wouldn't want to spoil our figures, now, would we?' As the girl grinned flirtatiously Leandro ignored her to instead rest his gaze very deliberately on Isabella, letting it slide libidinously down her body and back again. Witnessing her obvious discomfort, he shrugged almost arrogantly. 'That would indeed be a crime against nature…to spoil such beauty and perfection,' he commented, his voice seductively lowered. Wrenching her gaze free with difficulty, Isabella addressed her younger colleague in a sharper voice than usual. 'I'm sure you've got plenty to do before you leave at five-thirty, Becky, and so have I.'

She deliberately presented Leandro with her back to attend to some imaginary 'necessary' task, but not before she saw him push the envelope he'd written on further up the desk towards her…

CHAPTER FIVE

ISABELLA walked up and down the smart London street with its 'perfect' but way out of her price range terraced houses *twice* before plucking up the courage to ring the bell at the address that Leandro had given her. Number Sixty-six. Sixes and threes were always lucky for Isabella and she could certainly use some good fortune now, given the task ahead of her.

How would he take to the news that he was a father? Would he show her the door and tell her that he didn't want anything to do with either her *or* their child ever again? Isabella told herself that she was quite prepared for such an eventuality even though it would be dread-fully hard to bear. Leandro was, after all, no 'innocent' party she was wilfully trying to implicate. They had both had an equal part in creating Isabella's gorgeous little boy and it had been heartbreaking for her not to even be able to tell him about what had happened after she'd left the Port of Vigo and perhaps share the anxie-ties of her pregnancy and Raphael's birth with him—instead of going it alone all this time.

Well...she'd learned a tough lesson but Isabella

wasn't resentful. How could she be when she had Raphael? Motherhood had definitely changed her for the better and she'd met the challenges with courage and resourcefulness. And although admittedly in an ideal world it would have been preferable and perhaps easier to be part of a couple, she had nonetheless become a very capable single parent. So, it wasn't as though she *needed* Leandro's help or intervention, was it? She was merely going to tell him the truth at last. Even though she'd no doubt be emotionally crushed by his rejection when confronted with it face to face... 'Come on, Isabella, you can do this!'

Turning up the collar of her long winter coat to help fend off the freezing night air, she finally plucked up the courage to press the doorbell.

He had been like a man anticipating an urgent visit from his lawyer and a quick thankful release after being un-lawfully detained in prison—such was Leandro's impa-tience and insistent craving to see Isabella again. He could not remember the last time that he had done so much useless pacing in all his life! Picking up the screenplay that he had been in consultation with his script editor with for most of the morning, which—if he was honest—he was still vaguely unhappy with, he silently cursed his too distracted mind for making it almost impossible for him to concentrate. Rescuing the mug of strong black coffee that he'd made himself earlier, which was rapidly chilling since his thoughts had been so preoccupied, he settled himself deter-minedly in his friend Richard's agreeably comfortable high-backed armchair and struck his long legs out towards the fire blazing in the Edwardian fireplace. Resting his bare feet on the matching well-used footstool, he endeavoured to overcome his persistent preoccupation and try to relax instead. But it was just too hard to stop thinking about Isabella.

Seeing her at the library earlier had activated a need in him that he could scarce believe. Had he ever felt this agitated about seeing a particular woman before? He didn't think so... In fact nearly *all* of his previous girl-friends had accused him of being far too aloof and distant and not nearly as attentive as they would like...*including* the girl who had betrayed him with another man. When the doorbell sounded suddenly, chiming its incongruous cheerful tune throughout the house, Leandro bit back a relieved curse and levered his athletic frame with fluid ease out of his chair. Discarding the too cold mug of coffee on a small side-table, he drew in his breath and padded out in his bare feet to the sedately decorated corridor to answer the door. 'Sedate' because he'd wryly observed that the English seemed to have something against the use of bright vivid colour in their homes. Maybe it was something to do with the long months of 'grey' weather they had to endure?

Madre mia! Leandro's second sighting of Isabella's smiling but apprehensive beautiful face in the space of two short hours set his heart to racing. A surge of pleasure so profound captivating him, he found himself momentarily at a loss for words.

'Hello,' she greeted him softly, holding the collar of

her coat tightly together with one pale slim hand—her protective action and pinked cheeks reminding Leandro just how severely the temperatures had dropped since the morning.

'Isabella... Come in.'

Moving aside, he suddenly detected something different about her that he hadn't noticed before. What it was he did not know, because she was, in his eyes, lovelier than ever. As she passed him Leandro was aware of so many things about her that aroused him all at once. From the scent of the sharp cold air that clung to her clothing, to the deep sexy sheen of her blue-black hair beneath the hall light and her delicate, yet almost defiant jaw. A jaw that declared the señorita had claws beneath that deceptively sweet demeanour and should not be underestimated. Had he not had a glimpse of her temper in the library earlier?

Idly wondering how soon it would take him to turn that ignited passion to his own advantage should it arise again, Leandro could not help smiling in secret delectation at the libidinous nature of his thoughts. In the past eighteen months he had been around several lovely feminine creatures—mostly in the arena of his work— and *none* of them had had such a startling effect on his libido as this woman. In fact as Isabella brushed by him in the small compact hallway the heady pleasure that had mesmerised Leandro on immediate sight returned twice as vehemently. He cleared his throat as he shut the door behind them both, silently advising himself to rein in the trail of lust she unwittingly left in her wake.

'Turn to your left,' he instructed a little hoarsely. 'There is a fire in there to warm you.'

Surveying her with almost jealous possession as she went and stood near the fireplace and stretched out her hands towards the bright dancing flames, Leandro realised it was a supreme test of strength to tear his hungry gaze away for even a moment. It would have been entirely natural to perhaps assume that the time they had been apart had diluted the fierce attraction that Leandro had experienced towards Isabella practically on sight—but he was discovering to his immense satisfaction, that the *reverse* was true.

'You have no need of your coat now that you are inside. Here, let me take it.'

Before Isabella could properly compose her nerves, he was at her side, distracting her intensely with his disturbing presence. Her senses were immediately enraptured by the alluring warmth from his body and the disarming masculinity that electrified the air and seemed to be able to make her thoughts focus on not much else but sex. Her knees trembled as he dutifully waited for her to unbutton her coat and pass it to him. When she did, his returning, distinctly flirtatious glance kept her feet rooted to the floor. It was a wonder that smoke hadn't appeared! Now as she stood before him in the outfit she had so carefully selected to wear this evening to tell him her momentous news she worried that the plain black long-sleeved dress that skimmed her narrow waist and fell in fluid, easy lines to her knees was a little *too* severe. A little too staid and 'old maid-ish.' Well, it was too late now to do anything about it. All Isabella had been mindful of was dressing appropriately in deference to the gravity of what she had to reveal to Leandro.

When he returned from the hallway where he had briefly disappeared to take care of her coat, Isabella glanced quickly away from those 'heat-inducing' eyes of his with a jolt. The truth was, it was hard to rest her gaze for long on Leandro Reyes without feeling herself coming apart. He was so ruggedly handsome with his disreputably mussed dark hair and disturbing quicksilver gaze that a girl would have to have zero sex-drive and be deprived of all her senses not to be turned on by just the sight of him. The things an ordinary pair of softly faded denim jeans and a loose white shirt could do to that mouth-wateringly fit body of his, Isabella could wax lyrical about from here until the *next* millennium, given the opportunity! It was easy to see why she had succumbed so easily to his seduction last spring. Being in Northern Spain and experiencing the magic and allure of all that ancient land had to offer on the Santiago de Compostela trail had definitely helped. But, if she was entirely honest with herself, Isabella knew that Leandro Reyes would have been pretty much impossible to resist *wherever* she had met him. It was why she had fallen for him so hard and so fast...

'Why don't you sit and make yourself at home? What can I get you to drink?' There was an element of disconcerting amusement in his steady, intense regard and Isabella felt her cheeks shade helplessly scarlet in embarrassment. With his hands on his hips, he drew her very interested attention to that enviably easy way he carried himself and in the next moment she bypassed her self-consciousness to just simply gaze back at all that reined-in muscle and honest-to-God masculine beauty, with unconstrained appreciation. Then, guiltily tearing her gaze away, she glanced quickly round at the high-backed armchair beside the fire with its matching foot-stool. Her brows knit slightly as Leandro reached ahead of her and swiftly retrieved the sheaf of paper that was lying on the seat so that she could sit down.

'I have been working,' he explained, his expression serious as he laid the papers down on a cherrywood side-board instead.

'I haven't disturbed you?' Isabella responded with concern.

'Of course not.' He shrugged those wide shoulders of his with dismissive ease. 'I have been waiting impatiently for you to arrive.'

'And you are in London because of your work?'

'Not just because of my work,' he replied, 'although I have taken advantage of being here to meet with some people in my industry.' There was another conversation going on besides the one that traded actual words back and forth, Leandro considered as heat tightened his groin. They could hardly take their eyes away from each other. His skin felt hot...as though it were burning, and all he could really think about, focus on, was the arrestingly beautiful body beneath that funereal black dress she wore and how soon he might divest her of it to make love to her.

'But I do not want to discuss my work with you tonight, Isabella,' he told her out loud, his tone almost grave. 'As I already told you, that was not the main reason I came to the UK.'

'It wasn't?' In the armchair, Isabella carefully folded

her pale hands together in her lap, like a young girl about to solemnly take her first Holy Communion.

'I wanted to see you again. I should have contacted you before but there has been so much going on in my life in the past few months…' He shrugged, lifting his hands in a gesture to denote both inevitability and futility. 'I live a crazy life sometimes.'

'I realise that you must be a very busy man. But if you want to know the truth, it's a bit of a shock to have you make contact after this long.' Why had he come to find her at the library? Isabella fretted not for the first time. Was he hoping for a repeat performance perhaps of what they had shared in Spain? Her heart sank. As much as she cared for Leandro, she did not want to be used like that.

'But not an unpleasant shock, I hope?'

Was that doubt she saw briefly reflected in his hypnotic grey eyes? How could seeing him again be remotely unpleasant when she had dreamed of such a wonderful occurrence too many times to recall? Especially when their night together had produced her son? Which brought Isabella quite terrifyingly to the thing she most needed to discuss…the thing that was making her feel as if she were about to face a firing squad.

'No. Leandro…there's something that I must—'

'It was remiss of me not to give you my phone number,' he asserted firmly, 'but in my position it is not always easy to trust that people will have integrity and not abuse my trust. Do you understand?'

Isabella did. One could say that they had very similar 'issues' regarding trust and protecting their own privacy.

'Yes…' her gaze locked with his for terrifyingly long seconds '…I understand.'

'Now…before we go any further, naturally I want to know if you have been seeing anybody else since we last met? If not, then you must also tell me how it is that a beautiful, desirable woman like you has managed to stay unattached for so long?'

Her heart ached with gratitude that Leandro still thought her beautiful and desirable, but almost instantly Isabella returned to the most important part of his question, knowing she couldn't put off the answer for ever and wondering if his complimentary opinion of her might change when he heard the truth.

'No, I haven't been seeing anybody else. And there is a very good reason.'

Silence deepened the tension that was already holding Isabella's heart in a vice.

'And that reason *is,* Isabella?' Leandro prompted when she seemed not to be going to answer him at all.

'It's…' For goodness' sake, Isabella, just say it! 'It's complicated.'

'Then *enlighten* me, *por favor*?'

'All right…it's because I have a child to take care of.'

There…she'd said it and everything in the room looked just the same—even though everything had changed. Undoubtedly shocked, Leandro swept her with a blunt accusatory stare.

'You did not tell me when we met in Spain that you were a mother.'

Withdrawing his hand from his jeans pocket, he reached out to lean it on the marble mantelpiece instead.

He was more than a little stunned by Isabella's admission. He had of course known that she had previously been engaged because she had told him that she had cancelled her wedding—but he had not suspected for one moment that she might have had a child from that union! He wondered who had taken care of her or him whilst she had gone to Spain to walk the Santiago de Compostela. Was it the child's father? Five weeks was a long time for a child to be without its mother, in his considered opinion…

Her dark eyes troubled, Isabella released a long slow breath before getting to her feet. 'I *wasn't* a mother then,' she explained, folding her arms protectively across her chest. Absently she fingered the delicate gold crucifix that was attached to the slim chain she wore around her neck. She raised her chin a little at his frankly puzzled frown and pressed determinedly on. 'I had my baby nine months ago, Leandro…a little boy. His name is Raphael.'

'So you *did* meet someone else after we parted?' Barely registering that she had given her son a Spanish name, Leandro could not quell the sudden disturbing rush of fury inside his chest. Since that night he had spent with Isabella in her hotel, he had not slept with another woman. For a man with such a passionate nature, abstinence had been pure torture at times, but when opportunities had come his way he had rejected them—pure and simple—still too aroused by the memory of Isabella to do anything else. And yet, she had returned home to not only be with another man, but to have his baby as well!

'I…well, I—'

'So you and the child's father are no longer together?' he demanded, his throat dry as dust as he saw to his disappointment that she was finding it almost impossible to meet his eyes, an action that suggested that she was not being entirely honest. 'I distinctly recall you just telling me that you have not been seeing anybody else?'

'Leandro…' He saw her reach up and nervously smooth down her hair. He noticed her long ringless fingers and the indisputable elegance of her slim, pale hands. The same soft hands that had touched him and aroused his senses to a veritable inferno that long, hot, sultry Mediterranean night eighteen months ago… 'I told you the truth. I'm not seeing anyone else and I haven't *been* with anybody else since we were last together in Vigo! There's no other way I can put this to make it any less shocking but…the baby is *yours*, Leandro… *You're* his father.'

Hearing the words, Leandro had the strangest sensation that they were snatched up and thrown away by a great sandstorm that had suddenly appeared out of nowhere and had muffled his senses in the ensuing uproar. There was a lengthy stunned ellipsis in his thinking processes before he was able to assimilate their meaning fully into his consciousness. So preposterous was the mere *suggestion* that he could be the father of Isabella's baby that he sensed a mantle of ice engulf him, regarding her coldly as though she were suddenly an insignificant stranger to him. It might have been eighteen months ago since they had slept together, but Leandro knew without a doubt that he had used protection. He felt quite ill at the idea she was maybe using the opportunity of seeing him again to extract money or support from him for another man's child—particularly because he was wealthy.

'Impossible!' His dangerous grey eyes surveyed her with daggers so sharp that Isabella's heart was immediately pierced by his disbelief. Automatically her arms went back across her chest as if to fend off the rage that he directed her way. 'Do you take me for some ill-educated idiot? I could not possibly have made you pregnant, Isabella! You cannot be so forgetful as to remember that I used protection. What are you trying to do? *Blackmail* me in some way?'

'No!' Her dark eyes swam with vivid sparkling tears and inside Leandro felt as if he'd just been viciously winded by a hard punch. His hand was shaking as he tunnelled his fingers through his hair in justified frustration, refusing to be swayed by consideration of her hurt feelings when she clearly did not give a damn about his.

'I'm not lying to you, Leandro,' she insisted, rubbing at the moisture that glistened on her cheeks. 'I'll take any test you want me to take, but you are definitely the father of my child! And as for blackmail…well, that's a pretty hurtful accusation under the circumstances. I didn't *have* to come here… I could have stayed away and you would have been none the wiser about the baby. But when you turned up at the library like that and demanded that we talk, I *had* to tell you the truth, that's all. I naturally thought that you would want to know.'

'And how did we make a baby together when I

used contraception, Isabella? Or was it an *immaculate* conception?'

'Please, Leandro,' she pleaded through her tears. 'I'm telling you the truth, I swear it! It happened during the night...you—you reached out to me and I thought I was dreaming.' She dipped her head as a soft crimson stain crept into her cheeks. 'You obviously thought you were dreaming too. *That's* when it happened.'

An astounding, almost unbelievable memory flooded into Leandro's brain. For a moment it was hard to breathe. Isabella was *not* lying. Now that he'd been forced to remember the event in detail, he did recall reaching out to her at one point during that deliciously erotic night after they had both drifted into sleep. He even remembered thinking what an unbelievably realis-tic dream it was he was having because it was so real... He'd felt *everything*...her soft, full breasts, her smooth, flat stomach and, most of all, the searing hot wetness between her thighs as he'd so urgently plunged inside her... Now she was telling him that he'd fathered a child during that amazing night together...a boy...a boy called *Raphael*. All the moisture seemed to absent itself from Leandro's mouth at once.

'Why did you not try to get in touch with me when you found out that you were pregnant?' he asked hoarsely, his expression a vivid depiction of shock and pain.

'I did.' She met his gaze steadily for the first time in a couple of minutes without glancing away again. 'If you only *knew* how hard I tried! I tried every avenue I could think of...but the people who work for your film company clearly thought I was some kind of obsessive fan or something because they wouldn't even take a message, let alone give me a number to ring so that I could speak to you! I'm sorry, Leandro... I never wanted you to find out like this...to come face to face with the truth when I'd already had the baby and he was nine months old.'

'Why Raphael?' He moved across to the other side of the room and back, the tension in him reaching out to Isabella like icy tentacles wrapping themselves around her heart. 'Why did you call him that?'

'After my grandfather. His name was Raphael... Raphael Morentes. I told you he was Spanish?'

She had. But Leandro had scarcely given her an opportunity to tell him much about herself or her family that night. He had been concerned with one thing and *one* thing only: to fulfil the powerful lust she had ignited in him with her depthless black eyes and alluring body— not to mention revel in her exquisite sensitivity and unconstrained delight at his stories about the Camino... Now he'd learned that bedding Isabella had not only allowed him to fulfil his lustful attraction, but it had also produced a child...*his* child! It was an altogether incredible idea. He thought about his father Vincente and how long he had wanted Leandro to become a father too—to produce a grandchild for him to shower love upon. And for the past nine months, unknowingly to Leandro, he *had* become a father. Only Vincente had not lived long enough to see his grandchild.

For a moment, Leandro's heart cramped with searing emotion inside his chest. He had not even seen his own son yet... What did he look like? he wondered, dazedly glancing at Isabella again. Did he favour his mother or would he instantly see traits of his own familiar features? But before he met his son for the first time, Leandro needed some time to think about the momentous revelation of his existence. The most incredible thing had happened to him. He needed to sit down and think seriously about all the implications and about what steps to take next and he could not do that with the too-taunting distraction of Isabella. She would have to go.

'You will have to give me your address.' Diverting his glance, Leandro paced to a nearby table laden with books and papers. Picking up a pen and a sheet of paper, he returned to Isabella and handed them both to her. 'Write it down on there...your telephone number too...including your mobile, if you have one.'

Isabella was so upset by the coolly dispassionate glance he delivered her way that she saw her hand shake as she accepted the pen and paper. Did he think she was trying to ruin his life with her news of Raphael? That was the last thing she wanted! She had to make him see that she didn't blame him for getting her pregnant, that she loved her child with all her heart and would continue to take the very best care of him until he was grown—with or without his father's acknowledgment or presence in his life. But Isabella was hurt too...hurt that he seemed to be blaming *her* for getting pregnant when he was equally responsible. Carefully writing down her address and telephone numbers with a hand that could not cease its shaking, she handed the paper back to him in silence. He folded it in two and sighed deeply.

'*Gracias*. Now you should go.'

Stunned but not entirely surprised, Isabella smoothed her hands anxiously down the soft folds of her dress. Raising her eyes to his, she ventured softly, 'This isn't the end of your world, you know. You can carry on as normal if you like…you don't even have to stay in touch. I for one am so glad that I have Raphael and nothing will change my feelings on that score.'

He cursed. Out loud and in voluble Spanish. Isabella took a step back from the fury in his handsome face.

'You seriously believe that I am capable of calmly walking away from my own son when I have only just learned of his existence? Well, listen to this, Isabella, and listen *well*. It is *impossible* that I would even consider such a thing! Have you not heard of the word "honour" in your country? What kind of men are you used to seeing? Clearly the kind who know *nothing* of that word!' He took a deep despising breath and drove his hand with force through his already tousled hair. 'I will come and visit Raphael tomorrow at five o'clock when my business in town is concluded. Unfortunately I cannot put it off at this short notice even if I would like to, which I assure you I would.'

'You'll have to make it around six-thirty, not five,' Isabella said breathlessly, apprehensive of a further display of hot Latin temper. 'Raphael is at nursery until a quarter to six when I pick him up after work.'

'You have our nine-month-old son in a nursery?'

'I have to work, Leandro. How else do you think I support us?'

'He is clearly too young to be farmed out to strangers! What about your parents? Can they not take care of him while you are out at work?'

'No.' Swallowing hard, Isabella wondered how to explain to Leandro that, although her parents clearly did love their grandchild, they very much valued their own independence and would certainly not even remotely consider helping out with child-minding on a regular basis! 'I'm afraid they are not the kind of supportive parents that would do that.'

Leandro's expression was almost frighteningly forbidding. 'That is too bad,' he commented. 'We will clearly have to come to some far better arrangements for the future.'

She felt a bolt of alarm shoot through her at his ominous-sounding words, and Isabella's dark eyes cleaved anxiously to his resolute and steely glance.

'What do you mean by that exactly?' she demanded.

'We will discuss everything tomorrow,' he said firmly, absolutely refusing to be drawn.

Around six-fifteen the following evening, Isabella let herself hurriedly into her neat terraced house, flicked on the lights, raced straight through to the living room with her son fast asleep in her arms and laid him carefully down on the plump old-fashioned sofa with its loose floral cover. Stripping off her coat, she left it on a mismatched armchair bedecked with a maroon fringed shawl, then rushed back out into the hallway to turn on the central heating. The house was far too cold for comfort this evening. Or was that only because the blood in her veins kept turning to ice at the thought of what Leandro might be going to propose for their future? Hers and Raphael's?

The heating on, Isabella made her way into the kitchen, filled the kettle, found some cups and saucers, got the milk from the fridge, then returned to the living room to check on her infant. Raphael lay peacefully asleep, his plump, round cheeks rosy with health and his curly black hair made even more fetchingly tousled by his nap. Glancing across at the fringed shawl beneath her discarded coat, she stripped it off the chair and arranged it tenderly around her son. Softly, ever so gently so as not to wake him, Isabella touched her lips to his small downy cheek. Her heart squeezed with love. She would fight off rampaging lions with her bare hands to protect this child if it came to it.

Isabella didn't know what conclusions Leandro had reached about the situation now that he'd had time to consider it further, but whatever he'd decided, she consoled herself, he would have to consider her needs and wishes first. She might have identified him as the child's father when she'd registered Raphael's birth details with the authorities, but that still did not give him inalienable rights to dictate his son's future. They would have to discuss things in a calm, civilised manner and come to the best solution for all of them.

Determinedly dragging her thoughts away from possible disasters, she sighed, allowing her imagination to contemplate once again the full extraordinary reality of seeing Leandro yesterday. Coming face to face with him once more had been *wonderful* as well as nerve-racking because of what she had to tell him. Last night, sleep had mostly evaded her because her thoughts had been full of the memory of how good he had looked...how tanned and fit and *gorgeous*—that unusually light-coloured gaze of his sending hot sparks of delight and awareness to every corner of Isabella's being. And at least he had wanted to see Raphael... He hadn't rejected his existence outright as she'd secretly feared he might.

The ringing doorbell had her dashing out into the hallway and quickly checking her appearance in the mirror there as she passed. Grimacing that she hadn't even had a moment to pull a brush through her hair, she adjusted her sweater more smoothly over her breasts, absently ran her hands across her hips in smart black jeans, and just before she opened the door sent up a swift passionate prayer for courage and guidance. She had to tread carefully but firmly and make Leandro see that her main concern was her son's well being and not just her own. She would do nothing that would threaten his security in any way. It was vital that he recognised that. Now as Isabella saw him make a swift yet intense examination of her appearance as she opened the door—before greeting her with a very serious *'hola'*—answering heat assailed her body in a tumultuous rush. As well as stirring desire she didn't want to feel, it frustrated her like mad that she felt pretty damn defenceless when he looked at her like that—as though he was

mentally stripping her naked. And not just her body—
because it was as though all the contents of her heart and
mind were helplessly exposed to him too.

She wondered how on earth the actresses in the films
he directed managed to remember their lines when
Leandro gazed at them like that. Then she tried to quell
the hot flare of jealousy that exploded in her stomach
at the mere thought... Today he was wearing a clearly
expensive yet well-worn brown leather jacket opened
over a black cotton shirt with dark blue denim jeans.
With his dark hair edging onto his shoulders and his jaw
unshaven, his raffish appearance was more suggestive
of adventure and danger than 'ordinary' life as lived by
most people.

Isabella found herself wondering what her grandfather would have made of him. Would he have thought
Leandro a 'suitable' man to have a relationship with his
granddaughter and be the father of her baby? A stab of
sadness throbbed through her at the memory of the man
she had loved even more than the stepfather who had
helped raise her. The man who had even bequeathed her
his house so that she would never be without a home of
her own... Raphael Morentes was the kindest-hearted,
most loving man she had ever known. But Isabella also
reminded herself that a proper relationship with Leandro
was not really on the cards. They had slept together, yes,
and made a baby—but that did not mean that a fully
committed relationship naturally followed. Now she
was going to acquaint him with his son and that fraught,
no doubt emotive introduction was going to take every
ounce of her composure to help her get through it.

'You found us all right, then?'

She was papering over the cracks of her trepidation with inconsequential small talk and was not surprised when Leandro did not immediately answer. Stopping at the door of the living room, she gestured towards the kitchen. 'Shall we have a drink first? The weather is still so cold. You could probably do with a drink to—'

'I would like to see my son, Isabella,' he interceded clearly, his glance into her startled eyes unremittingly and disturbingly focused...

CHAPTER SIX

LEANDRO gazed down at his sleeping baby son with a fierce swell of pride, apprehension and love pouring through his chest all at the same time. The sensation rocked him so hard that the ground beneath his feet suddenly felt like the deck of a ship upon a wild, precarious ocean instead of the firm foundation he knew it was in reality. Tears stung his eyes as he dropped down onto his haunches, carefully smoothed back a rogue curl from the baby's velvet-smooth cheek and experienced the exquisite flutter of his gentle breath against his hand.

At thirty-six years of age, Leandro's life was not bereft of memorable moments, but this was one that would be recorded in the deepest annals of his heart, mind and soul for ever. Even with Raphael asleep, he had straight away recognised the similarity between his child and himself as an infant. Remembering his parents' photographs, he recalled that he had had the same black curly hair and the same plump features as the little boy before him. His mother would be undone by this news of a grandchild. Leandro could already imagine her weeping with joy. The baby's existence would help towards healing the great hurt done her when her beloved husband had lost his life so cruelly and without warning.

All at once he was galvanised by a tremendous sense of overwhelming purpose. The plans for the future that he had vaguely turned over in his mind last night after Isabella had left now became almost urgently reinstated at the sight of his child. He found that his thinking on the subject was so much more focused than it had been.

Surging to his feet, Leandro just about contained the sense of urgency that was gripping him to regard Isabella with deceptive calmness. She stood with her arms down by her sides, her face pale with anxiety, her dark eyes locking onto his as if she were a prisoner awaiting sentence and he the judge and jailer who held the key to her freedom or incarceration...

Attacked on all sides by a myriad conflicting emotions, Leandro clenched his jaw and drew determinedly upon his characteristic resolve to overcome the feelings that threatened to swamp him. Self-control was paramount now if he was going to achieve the outcome he suddenly knew with great clarity that he desired and he could not afford to be swayed by emotion alone. There were important things to be conveyed to Isabella...the mother of his son. Things that he had no time in which to consider how she would react to them, or whether they pleased or displeased her.

'I can see that he is my child...of that there is no doubt.' Moving his head slowly from side to side, Leandro took a moment to let the astounding realisation properly sink in. 'Last night, his existence was merely the most *impossible*, incredible idea. But now today, seeing him in the flesh…it is…' Dropping his hands to his hips, he looked nothing less than stunned. 'How can I explain? There are not the words to say.' As he considered Isabella his penetrating glance grew doubly resolute. 'But now that I have seen him…it is clear to me that you will both have to return to Madrid with me,' he declared, as though he were the authoritative captain of a ship announcing to his passengers that the crew had to make an unavoidable detour on their voyage…a detour that was *not* open to argument.

'What?' Now it was Isabella's turn to look stunned.

'I am due to start directing a new film in three days' time and I want you and our son with me when I return… I do not have time to contest this with you, Isabella; it simply *must* be. I have a house a little way from the old part of the town and fortunately I will be working close by because I am shooting on location there. There is no need to worry about bringing everything. Just pack essentials for you and the child for now. Anything else you want to bring I can arrange to have transported over later.'

Her mouth agape, Isabella closed it again as she strove to assimilate the sensation of being dragged along by a runaway train by her coat tails. Indignation helpfully shook her out of her temporary stupor. She could hardly believe what she was hearing. He wanted her and Raphael to move back to Spain with him in just a couple of days? As she considered the determined glitter in those incredible eyes of his, along with the indisputably dictatorial stance he was taking, Isabella inwardly took umbrage. 'Now wait a minute here! You can't just say, "It must be," and expect me to meekly agree as if there was no question that I should come with you! This is our home! My friends and my family live here... My life is here!'

'In Spain you told me that you wanted to live a different life. You said that things for you had become predictable...that you *longed* to change that. To me that would suggest that you might welcome the notion of living in another country—not be totally against the idea. Surely walking the Camino helped you to have less fixed and rigid views, Isabella?'

He had a point, of course. Feeling acutely discomfited by his solemn-faced cynosure as well as the wisdom in his words, Isabella sighed and ran her hand across her brow. 'My views aren't rigid or fixed!' she protested, glancing down at her slumbering baby. She had never sought to deny him knowledge or influence of his father—on the contrary, she had tried every which way she could to contact him—but at the same time Leandro could not just wade in and take charge of everything now that he was here. If only she could think more clearly for a minute! But that was easier said than done when the strongly magnetic pull for this man kept interfering—like some pirate radio station infiltrating the airwaves. 'But if you seriously expect me to consider your suggestion, then I need more than three days to think it over.'

'No,' he snapped back with a dangerously warning glance, 'that is not possible! I want my son with me when I return to Spain and I am not prepared to wait while you make up your mind about whether it is a good idea or not! How do I know that when I leave the country you would not flee somewhere else with Raphael and leave no forwarding address?'

Isabella blanched in indignation. 'I would never do that to you!' As she struggled to calm herself she could see the genuine fear in Leandro's expression that she might do just that and her heart turned over with sorrow. She would *never* deprive him of contact with his son or Raphael contact with his father. 'Look…this is an impossible situation. I know that. We *both* have to be reasonable if we're going to make the right decision…don't you agree?'

'The "right" decision?' For a moment Leandro appeared scornful. 'The right decision is that we simply have to do what is best for Raphael! And, in my opinion, living with *both* parents in a comfortable home and not lacking for anything is surely something to be desired and not rejected? Even if it is not in the country he was born in. I want to be in my son's life on a daily basis—I am not interested in a long-distance "weekend father" kind of relationship! The only way we can accomplish that is for both of you to come and live with me. I say again, Isabella…it is *Raphael's* welfare that must take precedence over any other considerations. And I have already been deprived of nine months of his life and do not intend to be deprived of any more!'

At the sound of the raised male voice, Raphael stirred where he lay on the sofa beneath the pretty fringed shawl, opened his startling grey eyes and whimpered softly as he looked up at Leandro.

'*Increíble...*'

Lapsing into awed Spanish, Leandro gazed down into the glistening mirror of his infant son's eyes, his expression rapt. Any vestige of doubt that they were father and son was annihilated into dust in that amazing moment. He let his breath out slowly.

Automatically moving past him to pick up her infant, Isabella felt her own body tremble violently with emotion. She felt for both of them. For her baby son who, did he but know it, was looking upon the face of his father for the very first time...and for Leandro, meeting the child he hadn't even known existed until yesterday...

I have already been deprived of nine months of his life and do not intend to be deprived of any more!

The ache inside her throat burned intolerably as Leandro's passionate words echoed hurtfully round her brain. She had tried so hard to contact him when she'd found out that she was pregnant, but every avenue, every door to reaching him, had been absolutely shut in her face. It would have been easier to try and make contact with the Pope! What was she supposed to have done under the circumstances but decide to raise her child on her own?

Frustration and guilt gripping her, Isabella tried to stay calm for her son's sake. Carefully lifting Raphael up into her arms, she cradled him tenderly as he laid his head on her shoulder and proceeded to suck his thumb— all the while regarding Leandro from beneath his sable lashes with a mixture of curiosity and wariness.

'He's hungry,' Isabella declared tightly as she walked back across the room and out into the kitchen. Retrieving a bottle of milk formula from the fridge, she opened the microwave, tapped in the correct heating time and switched it on. As the plate inside started to rotate with the bottle of milk, she turned round to find Leandro framed in the doorway, his expression bordering on accusatory as his gaze met hers across the distance between them. 'You are not feeding our son yourself?'

For a second or two Isabella froze. Then as another guilty wave immersed her, she bit back the angrily defensive retort that she'd been about to let loose. Instead she started to pat Raphael comfortingly on the back as, sensing her discomfort, he began to struggle in her arms.

'No…I'm not. I breastfed him for three months but it was difficult.' Leandro's steady gaze held hers in thrall and for a tense, troubling moment Isabella could not break free from the spell. Feeling his scrutiny and judgement intensely, she started to rock rhythmically from side to side in a bid to comfort her increasingly restless baby son. It was clear to her that Raphael could absolutely sense her unease and the effect this 'strange' man was having upon his mother's usual calm. 'I was suffering with post-natal depression for a while and my milk just seemed to—to dry up,' she continued with her explanation.

The words seemed as insubstantial as cotton wool— as though she were merely making unconvincing excuses for what Leandro must see as her complete lack of determination in the matter. Isabella could have cried with the deep unfairness of his perceived judgement. It had not been easy being pregnant and having to cope with the prospect and reality of bringing a child into the world on her own. Apart from the physical aspects, emotionally Isabella had not known what had hit her. And when she hadn't even been able to contact Leandro to let him know what had happened after their night together, she had experienced overwhelming fear and the most devastating vulnerability too. Swallowing hard, she jiggled Raphael some more to get him to settle but he would not be comforted. He was as mesmerised by Leandro as she was and kept straining to look at him over her shoulder.

'You should have had proper help so that you could continue. In Spain we would have done things properly.'

The accusation in his voice no longer open to speculation but just about as obvious as it could get, Leandro walked towards her and held out his arms. 'Give him to me,' he ordered quietly. Wanting to resist but somehow unable to, Isabella relented, and surprisingly Raphael immediately quieted. Her heartbeat slowed to an astonished thud inside her chest. Jerking his head a little towards the microwave, then looking straight at her, Leandro positioned his hands securely around his baby son and held him tenderly to his chest. 'See to the milk. I will take Raphael into the living room and we will wait for you.' Breathing out with some force as they left the room, Isabella heard the timely 'ping' from the microwave and, opening the door, reached inside in a daze to retrieve the now-warmed milk...

'*Soy su padre, mi hijo.*' I am your father, my son... The rest of the world retreated into oblivion as Leandro spoke to his child alone for the first time and he was completely content just to let it. The concerns that had lately been so prevalent and that had seemed to tirelessly dominate his thinking—his father's death, his mother's melancholy, the unsatisfactory script for the new film, even his increasing desire to see Isabella again—all stole into a silent void as he willingly lost himself in the wide grey innocent eyes that solemnly gazed up at him. The one thought that did consume him was that in the instant he had glanced back into that curious and innocent glance Leandro *knew* that he had become the fiercely protective custodian of this beautiful innocent life he held in his arms. He would willingly die before he let harm touch so much as one hair of his son's head. That being the case, Isabella had no choice but to return to Spain with him and their son. Any arguments she put to him to dispute that choice, Leandro would ruthlessly knock down as easily as a pack of cards. But he *would* get his way…he *had* to get his way. He owed it not just to himself, but to the memory of his beloved father who had longed for the miracle Leandro held in his arms right now. *Raphael*…his perfect little son…

'Let me take him.'

Suddenly Isabella was there, regarding Leandro with apprehension and concern in her dark-eyed glance as she approached him—clearly oblivious to anything else but the beautiful child he held in his arms.

'I can feed him.'

He held out his hand for the bottle of milk she had brought and felt a flash of irritation ricochet through his insides when she seemed to hesitate. 'Do you not think I know how to handle a little one like this? Give me the milk and you can go and take a bath or do whatever it is you need to do to help you relax after work.'

Surprised to say the least by his apparent considera-tion of her own possible needs, Isabella handed Leandro the bottle and watched him position the teat in Raphael's eager little mouth—her son clearly displaying no protest at having his father feed him instead of his mother. They looked quite at home, the pair of them—as though this were a ritual they shared on a nightly basis instead of it being the very first time... Isabella couldn't deny the odd mix of confusion and yet delight that was generated inside her at the touching sight.

'I'm famished and I was going to get something ready for dinner... You're welcome to join me if you haven't eaten yet.' He'd probably refuse, she told herself. And it would be nothing less than idiotic to feel rejected if he did. But right now no amount of sensible advice she could offer herself was likely to help. Not when her feelings about this man were all tangled up with her quite tangible fears about her own and her baby's future.

'How could I possibly refuse such a lovingly extended invitation?' he responded mockingly. To Isabella's intense alarm, Leandro glanced up at her with the kind of taunting, devilish sparkle in his striking gaze that could make a woman lose the power of speech and she recalled just how receptive she'd been to those scorching little glances when he'd first employed them and she had ended up in bed with him. That never-to-be-forgotten event that had resulted in the adorably sweet child he now cradled in his arms.

'I was only going to make a simple rice dish so don't get your hopes up. I'll feed Raphael his meal first, then I'll bath him and put him to bed. After that we can eat and talk… That is if you're not in a hurry to go anywhere else for a while?'

'Is it likely that I would be in a hurry to go somewhere else tonight, Isabella?'

The smile that had touched his lips and caused such mayhem vanished, and the look he levelled at Isabella instead was as devoid of humour as a judge at the Old Bailey presiding over a murder trial. Immediately she mourned for his smile.

'We need to talk and discuss our plans for the future. I am not going anywhere until we have those firmly in place…and I am warning you now that I will *not* be taking no for an answer when it comes to the matter of you and Raphael coming to live in Madrid with me.'

'You can't make a contentious statement like that and expect me to—'

'I am afraid I *can*…but before you say anything else there is something I have to ask you.'

'What's that?' Forced to curtail her annoyance and not happy about it one iota, Isabella crossed her arms over her chest and inwardly seethed.

'Your family…do they know that I am Raphael's father?'

The question completely took the wind out of Isabella's sails. It was a great sadness to her that she had not been able to share her child's father's identity with anyone…not even her own mother. How many times, when people had expressed admiration for her beautiful son's 'amazing' eyes or stunning face, had she had to suppress her longing to say, Yes, he is so like his father. His name is Leandro Reyes and he is amazing too.

Emilia had done her best, of course, to try and get her to confess the identity of Raphael's father, but Isabella instinctively knew the potential danger of such a confession to a woman as ambitious as her sister. The last thing she wanted either for herself, Raphael *or* Leandro was some glib article about them featuring in Emilia's magazine. And if by some unbelievable fluke it had been mooted by someone else that Leandro Reyes might well be the father of Isabella's son, then Emilia—perversely, she was sure—would be the first to deny such an implausible premise. Because in her eyes *she* was the beautiful, successful daughter in the family who consorted with the rich and famous...*not* Isabella...

'No,' she said out loud in answer to Leandro's question. 'None of them know. I thought it best under the circumstances not to tell them.'

Because perhaps she viewed their lovemaking as an unimportant one-night stand that she'd succumbed to whilst away from home in a strange country? The thought was like the tip of a red-hot poker suddenly pressed against Leandro's skin. But then he regrouped. Had Isabella resisted naming him as Raphael's father to her family because of the celebrity attached to his name? Did she think that perhaps they would not believe her story or that they might even press her to pursue him for support? In other words...had she been protecting *him*?

'Why?' he asked her, moving Raphael closer into

his chest and revelling in the strong feelings of protectiveness and warmth that deluged him. 'Were you
ashamed of what happened?'

'No!'

The passion in her face reassured Leandro that his
initial speculation was wrong even more convincingly
than her fierce denial. He felt himself relax against the
back of the sofa and even briefly smiled. 'Then why?
Why did you not tell them that I was Raphael's father?'

'Why should I? I'm an adult…and what I do is *my*
business, not theirs.' Isabella would not go on to explain
to him that whatever decisions or actions she took—they
were nearly *always* criticised by her exacting parents.
Therefore, telling them about Leandro would only have
invited more condemnation and disapproval, and,
honestly, what self-respecting, intelligent human being
would welcome that? Sighing, Isabella moved grace-
fully across the room to absently straighten one of the
silver-framed photographs on the window sill.

Waiting patiently for her further explanation, Leandro
was quite content to observe her eye-catching curves in
her slim black jeans and agreeably tight sweater. With
her long dark hair reaching down to the middle of her
back and the too-distracting sway of her hips when she
moved, she was the kind of earthy, sexy woman whose
arousing image would disrupt most men's sleep when
they saw her. Registering the inevitable tension that this
thought produced, Leandro tried to will away the passionate arousing memory of that long hot night they'd
spent together in Spain, but he wasn't strong enough to
totally banish the image that taunted him.

'Anyway…I don't want anyone knowing my business except those I know I can really trust…and unfortunately they are few and far between. And you must have enough to contend with already being in the public eye without having stories about an illegitimate son appearing in the papers.'

Staring down at the near blissful expression on Raphael's face as he continued to drink from his bottle, Leandro admired Isabella's obvious integrity at wanting to protect her own *and* his privacy, but he winced at the repugnant idea of his child being labelled 'illegitimate' in the newspapers… His father, Vincente, would turn in his grave! Which immediately presented him with another dilemma that needed resolving. This particular one he decided to save until they got the chance to talk properly later…but he vowed that after the matter of Isabella moving out to Spain with him, it would be top of his agenda.

'But you say you tried to contact me when you found out that you were pregnant?' He lifted his gaze as she slowly walked back across the room towards him, unable to stop himself from appreciating the very arresting picture she made. *Dios mio!* But she was more bewitching than any sultry movie star he had ever worked with!

Recalling the painful memory of being so clearly disbelieved at claiming acquaintance with Leandro… not just once, but *several* times by the different people at his film company's offices, Isabella frowned. 'I tried many times, Leandro…but I think your people truly believed that I was some kind of stalker or something!

Anyway...they wouldn't take a message no matter how many times I rang, and all my letters went unanswered. I suppose it comes with the territory when you're well known and don't know who you can trust...but it made it impossible for me to let you know about Raphael.'

'So—' Leandro lowered his voice with the heaviest of sighs '—you thought that you would never see me again?'

'Can you blame me for thinking that? On the morning we said goodbye it was "business as usual" for you—I could tell you'd probably never even give me another thought once I was gone!' She shrugged, her heart filling with renewed hurt that he could dismiss so casually what they'd shared. It hadn't helped when a woman at his offices had made some exasperated comment when Isabella had phoned, that Leandro Reyes *always* had some woman hanging on his coat tails!

'It is not true that I did not think of you again. Why do you think I am here now?'

Isabella didn't answer him that she'd privately speculated that he was looking for another one-night stand. She was too upset to even say the words. Turning away so that he wouldn't witness the tears that had momentarily clouded her vision, Isabella went to the door. 'I should get on and get some dinner ready. Are you all right holding the baby for a while? You can lay him down on the sofa if he gets too heavy.'

She disappeared before Leandro could even reply...

As they sat in Isabella's small, neat kitchen to eat the meal she had prepared and served—Raphael sleeping peacefully in his bed after his bath and some rhythm and blues music station playing quietly in the background on the radio—Isabella stole a glance at the man sitting opposite her across the Spanish lace tablecloth she'd brought back from Santiago. There were so many topics she'd love to converse with Leandro about besides the astounding fact that they had a son together. He was an amazing man doing extraordinary work in a field of the arts that people were fascinated by and she longed to tell him how much she had loved the film he'd directed that she'd seen the other night with Chris. But, although right now there was little distance between them physically, emotionally they seemed miles apart. Leandro Reyes was an unknown quantity to Isabella even though her feelings for him were not, and she longed to find a way to bridge that seemingly enormous gulf between them. He apparently loved his son on sight, but would that be enough to cement a proper relationship between him and Isabella and was that what he really wanted?

Guiltily catching his eye and seeing him offer a wry smile, Isabella sighed out loud and put down her fork. The poor man had just discovered she wasn't exactly a gourmet cook. It was fairly evident that the dish she had cooked was pretty inedible. But how was she supposed to be able to concentrate on cooking when the father of her child—a man she had only met twice before and had experienced the most momentous connection with— was sitting in her living room cradling their child as if he were the pivot on which the earth turned round?

'I'm sorry…this is pretty awful. You don't have to eat it.'

'No…it is fine. I am not so hungry anyway. It is not the food that I came here for, Isabella, as we both know…'

She knew that he was talking about the baby but the intensity of his gaze was like coming into direct and sudden contact with the relentless reflection of a glaring Spanish sun and Isabella pushed back her chair a little too suddenly and got to her feet. Moving across to the clean granite worktop next to the fridge, she took the cork out of the bottle of red wine that resided there and poured Leandro a generous glassful, then a much smaller one for herself. Bringing the glasses to the table, she sat back down again and smiled awkwardly.

'Perhaps this will get rid of the taste,' she joked, raising her glass to her lips and taking a sip. The alcohol acted like a heady cocktail to her already heightened nervous system, but Isabella told herself she needed some kind of boost to help her deal with the discussion that was about to take place.

'Isabella?'

'Yes?'

'Let us not waste any more time with distracting trivialities. We need to talk seriously.'

'Yes, I know that.'

She wouldn't look into his eyes, she vowed nervously. Leandro Reyes was possessed of the kind of eyes that stole a woman's soul and haunted her for ever and she needed to stay strong and focused—not just for her own sake, but for Raphael's too.

'You realise that you are going to have to agree to be my wife?' he said commandingly before he leant back in his chair and sighed heavily. 'Don't you?'

CHAPTER SEVEN

SHE was so amazed by this statement that for a moment all Isabella could do was stare at Leandro blankly as she strove to get her astounded brain to deal with what she'd just heard. Was he joking? There was no smile touching his lips, no humorous glint in his eye. She had to assume he was serious.

'But I don't want to get married!' she said in agitation, rising to her feet.

Leandro kept his features perfectly neutral as he too stood up, but inside his chest his heart had jolted in surprised protest at her point blank refusal of the suggestion he had made. Was it marriage in general she had something against or was the idea of marrying him simply one she could not entertain? For a moment, the latter thought made his blood throb with anger. He didn't think he'd be overstating the matter if he concluded that most women he met considered him a more than reasonable catch. But not *this* woman, apparently. When he had discovered yesterday that Isabella had had his baby, his natural inclination had been to make her his wife and that was still

Leandro's goal. He simply would not entertain the idea of his son's parents living apart from each other whilst he was growing up. Leandro had seen the effects of separation on too many of his friends' children to be at all enamoured of the idea—no matter what the reasons.

'We have to think of the child,' he insisted, grey eyes turning to flint. 'It is in Raphael's best interests that he has a mother and father who are together and married, rather than he lives with just one of us alone. Living in England is not an option for me, seeing as most of my film work is in Spain. It is simply not practical that we live together here. The other important consideration is that my family live in Madrid…as I do. When they find out about Raphael they will naturally want him close by so that they can see him regularly.'

'And what about *my* family?'

'You have already more or less indicated that you are not close.' Shrugging his broad shoulders with arrogant ease, Leandro dismissed Isabella's comment as being of little to no account. She had a pushy sister, as he recalled, who had insensitively persuaded her against her will— whilst she had been undertaking a quest of her own— to try and find him and gain an interview, and a mother and father who did not sound like the most loving of grandparents that a child could wish for. Parents who could not find it in their hearts to help their daughter with childcare when she was clearly in need hardly *deserved* consideration as far as he was concerned. He knew his mother, aunts and extended family would feel exactly the same dismay about them as he did. In fact it was quite detestable to Leandro to think of his son in the sphere of such aloof and perhaps cold people.

The spread of crimson on Isabella's otherwise pale cheeks spoke volumes, but he would not let her discomfort at his frankness sway him. Right now he was more interested in persuading her to concede to his very justified demand that she and Raphael return to Spain with him. And as far as their future relationship was concerned, well... Leandro was absolutely adamant that they *had* to get married for Raphael's sake.

'And besides that—you forget that I have a job here. A job that I really do enjoy,' she elaborated.

'And this is the same job that you told me you had become dissatisfied with?'

The sarcasm in his tone deepened Isabella's blush. 'I was able to look at it in a more positive light when I returned from Spain!'

'And so...does it pay good money, this job you are suddenly so eager to stay with?'

'That's none of your business!'

'I beg to disagree. It is very *much* my business when it concerns my son's welfare.'

Isabella glared. 'We do all right...and my grandfather left me this house so at least I have no mortgage to pay. I've also been working really hard towards getting a promotion and that means a pay rise, so financially things will be a lot easier for us then.'

'I am sorry but I cannot say that fills me with confidence, Isabella. If you are struggling to manage on one wage then you are clearly *not* doing all right! And unless your expected promotion pays you double what you

earn already—then in my opinion you will *still* be struggling to make a decent standard of living. There is
simply no good reason for you to remain here in
England when you and Raphael can live very comfort-
ably with me in Spain. Besides, do you not realise you
will have a job that you really enjoy there too?'

A smile tugging at the corners of his mouth, Leandro
closed the distance between himself and Isabella—his
previous irritation stunningly transformed into a commanding need for intimacy that was so all-pervasive
and persuasive that for a moment he completely forgot
his impatience with her. Her arresting scent clung to the
air with hypnotic sweetness and those disturbingly dark
eyes with their lush ebony lashes rendered him more
captivated than any acknowledged beauty in the film
industry he had ever worked with.

'You will be able to be at home with Raphael full
time, and when you want a break my mother and my
aunts will no doubt offer their services. You will not
have to juggle both work and childcare like you are
doing now and you will have more free time to pursue
other interests as well. Speaking of other interests…what about your book? The one you were writing
about the Camino? How close are you to finishing it?'

It was hard to formulate an answer to the question
when he was standing so near. And Isabella was still
trying to come to terms with his stunning suggestion of
getting married. This was Leandro Reyes she reminded
herself with a powerful sense of shock shooting through
her veins—world-renowned film director and much
admired by many… This was no simple love affair with

a handsome stranger. It had connotations that were both life-changing and far-reaching. She could be laying her whole life open to public scrutiny for one thing…*especially* if she agreed to marry him. Being a person who liked to safeguard her privacy as much as possible, the very idea of being so exposed was anathema to her. Brushing her hair behind her ear with her fingers, Isabella forced herself to meet the mercurial gaze that so mercilessly dazzled her.

'I've still got quite a way to go. I just haven't really been able to find the time… I do intend to finish it, though. I think about it often.'

It was true. Isabella also thought about the momentous few weeks she'd walked the Camino trail and what it had meant to her personally. As well as the physical challenge and the profound personal transformation, her senses had been confounded with secret delight by all the sights and sounds she'd been greeted by in that part of Spain. The architecture, the history, the wild landscapes and the amazing people she'd met would be with her for ever. And those people—her fellow *peregrinos*—had all bar none accepted her just for herself. There had been no judgement and no expectation involved, just simple, uncomplicated companionship and friendship, and it had been such a relief. Coming from the family she did, where conformity to their wishes and expectations was an ever-present challenge, walking the Camino had helped give Isabella back her sense of herself.

Since her return she'd vowed not to relinquish that sense of self to anyone else's desires ever again. But most of all…most of all she remembered that never-to-be-forgotten meeting with Leandro and the magical evening they had shared that had started out in Señor Varez's little bar and ended up in a hotel room that was the height of luxury. The still air had bathed them in sultry heat and their only accompaniment had been the music of the rain that had hypnotically glanced against the windows. Together they had turned that night into a spellbinding dream… Meeting Leandro had changed everything for Isabella. Apart from her knowing that she could never give her heart to any other man but him, he had given her her beautiful baby son. Now no one would ever convince her that there was no such thing as divine intervention…

'Then you must finish it when you come to Spain, no?' His warm fingers glancing against the underside of her chin came as the most exhilarating thrill and Isabella found herself catching her breath as heat flooded through her in an intoxicating rush. 'Never underestimate the importance of art,' he asserted huskily. 'It is the secret to saving our sanity in this world. But it will be easier for you to think about this when there is no longer the need to go out to work.'

Although his encouraging words about art—in her case writing her book—were music to Isabella's ears, the tacit implication in Leandro's words told her that he already believed he had her full agreement to go to Spain and live with him, and that was *not* a decision that she had definitely reached at all. It made her panic a little. Especially when she believed that he was only asking her because of his deep sense of responsibility towards Raphael. What if the profound connection she had sensed between them had been one sided? She did not know as yet what Leandro really felt about her at all. And she still couldn't help wondering if he had only looked her up because he was in London and saw an opportunity for another hot little encounter with her. Now, because of their son, he was saddled with a woman for whom the only feelings he entertained might be purely sexual. Hurt and disappointment welling up inside her, Isabella knew she could not remotely consider marriage with this man if he didn't love her.

'I'm sorry, Leandro, but I'm overwhelmed by what you expect me to do! First you insist that we move to Spain with you practically immediately, then you tell me that we must get married ! You say that it's in Raphael's best interests that we make a life together, but can you really be so sure that that's what's best? What if him being here with me and seeing you whenever you can make it to England would be the best thing for him? He's happy at his nursery. It's run by a very close friend of mine and I *know* that she ensures he has the best care. As for us...' The skin between Isabella's dark brows puckered a little as she contemplated the thing that was disturbing her the most. 'We slept together once and we made a baby. That doesn't mean that we could make a marriage between us work *or* that we'd be better parents if we were together. What I think is that we both need more time to really work this out...to come up with the best solution. Don't you agree?'

Her plea for understanding did not elicit the positive response she might have hoped for. To her shock and surprise Leandro abruptly turned and walked away from her, but not before Isabella registered the volatile spark of fury and impatience in his eyes with a nervous somersault in her stomach.

'I cannot give you more time!' he declared, turning to face her again. 'Have you not been listening? I already told you that I needed to be back in Madrid in three days' time. I do not have the kind of job where I can get someone to stand in for me when I take time out... I have an expensive cast and crew waiting for me when I get back that expect me to be there on schedule to start shooting this film, not to mention the financial backers who expect one-hundred-and-ten-per-cent commitment for the money they are investing. So you see, Isabella, I cannot wait for you to make up your mind to come to Spain with me. Raphael is *my* son too and I want full custody of him alongside his mother! To lose nine months of my child's life is bad enough—to lose even *one* more day of that life is inconceivable to me now that I have seen him and held him in my arms. Can you not comprehend that?'

As well as being furious at her seeming obstruction of his desires, simmering deep inside Leandro was absolute rage that he had not received any of Isabella's messages about her pregnancy. When he got back to Madrid, one of the first tasks he would be undertaking was to call on the film offices concerned, make a proper investigation about what had happened and then make his fury known to the people responsible. Their over-zealous protection had denied him knowledge of his son as well as the once-in-a-lifetime chance to witness the miracle of his birth, and to his mind that was *not* an action that would be eliciting his unconditional forgiveness any time soon...

'Of *course* I can comprehend that you want to be with your son, Leandro, but sometimes it's just not possible to have our desires instantly gratified. Sometimes a little planning and forbearance is required.'

'*Dios mio!* You test *my* forbearance, Isabella!'

His white-hot anger cut Isabella to the quick. This was definitely *not* the kind of reunion she would have envisaged for them both, given the choice. Now she felt utterly miserable.

'You have no idea what it means to me to discover I have a son...no idea at all.' His lean jaw visibly clenched, Leandro focused his agitated gaze firmly on Isabella's unhappy face. 'It is punishment enough that I did not know of his existence until yesterday. Do not punish me further by keeping him from me another day.'

As she heard the anguish in his voice Isabella's heart ached for his distress. Now she knew an instinctive need to hold him, to tell him she understood his great need to be around his child...but, fearing that he might reject such advances when the atmosphere between them was fraught with such tension, she stayed where she was, her arms down by her sides.

'My father died.'

'What?' Isabella held her breath in surprise and shock. She saw Leandro lift up his hand to push it through his hair, but he stopped halfway and shook his head, as if it pained him beyond measure to even say the words. 'When?' she asked him. 'When did this happen?'

'Not long after we said goodbye in Vigo. He was mowed down by a drunken driver... It is also why I need to be with my son.'

Sensing that he did not want to go into detail, Isabella felt her heart swell with compassion. Now she understood why he was so vociferous about his demands that they go to Spain. If he had recently lost his father...and in such a *brutal*, shocking way...it must be even more important for him to have a close bond with his son.

'I'm so sorry, Leandro.' She moved towards him to touch him, to show him how moved she was by his confession, but he stepped away from her, as if he almost regretted having to share this information with her. His gaze glittered fiercely.

'I do not need your sympathies, Isabella!' he said savagely, and a muscle ticked at the side of his lean jaw. 'All I need is for you to come to Spain with Raphael!'

Leandro had not wanted to tell Isabella about what had happened to his father, but the emotion of their situation had prised the information from him. He only hoped that he could trust her not to share it with anybody else. He was fiercely protective of his especially close relationship with his father, even more so since he had gone. His reasons for wanting Isabella to move to Spain with him were imperative and he was not playing games here. He wanted Raphael with him...he wanted his *son*. He could not go home without him now that he had seen him. He owed it to Vincente to be a good father to his grandson—the way Vincente had been a good father to

Leandro. What he could not afford to do was let Isabella's doubts cloud the issue in any way.

'Leandro? Raphael's happiness and well-being means everything to me and I don't want to do anything to jeopardise that. If I come to Spain with you, I need to feel that I'm doing the best thing for my son…that I won't regret it.'

He stared at her as though it pained him to look at her. 'Put yourself in *my* position—a father who did not know he was a father until yesterday, nine months *after* my son was born—and then you will know about regret, *querida*…'

And without another word he left her there alone in the kitchen, his expression an amalgam of sorrow and anger as he furiously brushed past her, leaving Isabella feeling as if she'd done him the most dreadful wrong that she might never be able to put right….

Leandro ended the conversation with his mother and placed the receiver back on its rest. His hand shook slightly as he did so. After getting over the initial shock, Constanza Reyes had been ecstatic to learn that he had a son and that he was bringing him home with him tomorrow. She had laughed and cried for joy, as well as pledging to offer prayers to the saints, and the terrible depression that had descended upon her since his father's death had seemed to miraculously recede. For such a blessing, Leandro knew only the most unimaginable gratitude. But strangely enough the conversation had left him a little morose instead of completely happy. He had lost a father and gained a son, but relations with the woman who was the mother of his child were under a most regrettable strain. Isabella had been on his mind almost constantly since he had left her last night—as indeed she had been on it over the past eighteen months—and he longed to know how to make relations between them more conducive.

Was he so wrong to expect her to leave her life in England and make a new life with him and Raphael in Spain? After the time they had spent together in the Port of Vigo last spring, Leandro did not think that he had imagined the powerful connection that had radiated so compellingly between them. When he had let Isabella go without even giving her his cell phone number, he had had much cause to regret his overly cautious action. And all that time after she had left she had been pregnant with his child and he had not known it… Regret and pain locked his throat when he considered how she had managed on her own and how betrayed she must have felt when the film company would not even pass on her messages to him. He should not be surprised that any vestiges of past affection had probably been obliterated under the circumstances.

Yet he could not help craving her attention like a drug he could not give up. Last night he had slept little. How could a man sleep when he was plagued by day-dreams and fantasies of a woman who fulfilled every criteria of feminine perfection that Leandro could imagine? The softly provocative kisses he had received from her delectable lips in that hotel room eighteen months ago—as well as the memory of the arousing little sounds she had made in the throes of making love—were a seductive torment to him even now in the cold light of morning.

Impatiently he pushed to his feet, driving his hands into the slim pockets of his jeans as once again the hot, drugging heat that flooded his body at the thought of Isabella made it impossible to sit or relax at all. As his edgy, preoccupied gaze swept the newly tidy room that his friend's housekeeper had restored in the early hours whilst Leandro had been working he had to console himself with the fact that at least tomorrow he would have the chance to be alone with Isabella and Raphael in his *own* house. And once his baby son was fed and settled for the night, then he would waste no more time in making relations between himself and his beautiful *amante* far sweeter and more agreeable than they were at present. And living with him and sharing some of the material and cultural advantages of his world and seeing how much that environment must benefit their son, Isabella would soon forget her worries that she might be jeopardising Raphael's happiness and quickly agree to becoming Leandro's wife…

CHAPTER EIGHT

THEY arrived at Leandro's house in Madrid some time in the early evening when dusk was approaching. Not knowing his personal tastes at all, Isabella was struck by the quiet, unpretentious beauty of the stone-built farmhouse—known as a *finca* in Spanish, as Leandro had informed her—situated far away from the hub of the main town in rural splendour. Its edifice glowed cloud-white in the fading light of day and as they drove up in the car Leandro had left at the airport for his return the external lighting automatically came on, illuminating their way. Almost immediately there was something about the place that touched a chord deep inside Isabella. An inexplicable sense of coming home even though she told herself she was just being ridiculous and foolishly, unrealistically hopeful. Deliberately, she put the feeling aside.

She shivered slightly in the cool night air as she stepped out of the car, her senses immediately capti-vated by the richly resinous scent of the earth, and her blood was irrevocably stirred. She *loved* this land, she realised. She had grown up loving it because of her wonderful grandfather who had told her so many stories about his homeland that it had almost made Isabella homesick. That was why she had always longed to walk the Camino. Somehow, undertaking such a pilgrimage had brought her even closer to the spirit of her grandfather as well as to the land, and it had also set her on the way to discovering what was her own heart's desire.

Flicking a quick covetous glance at Leandro as he walked round to the boot of the car to see to their luggage—his long-legged stride and broad shoulders in his stylish sports jacket and jeans making her heart race suddenly—Isabella reflected that perhaps it hadn't been so difficult for her to make the decision to come back to Spain after all.

'He is asleep?'

'Yes…he hardly even put up a fight. I think the plane journey and the travelling wore him out.'

'Sí…I think you are right.'

Immediately detecting the apprehension in her expression that she could not hide, Leandro wondered how Isabella had viewed the fact that he had moved her immediately into the master bedroom—her cases down by his next to the big brass and iron bed that he usually slept in alone. They were going to be man and wife…and he saw no point in delaying the inevitable and making her doubt his intention by giving her a room of her own. Especially not when he had already waited eighteen months to experience the rapturous feeling of her body next to his again.

Raphael's travelling cot, Leandro had placed next to

Isabella's side of the bed until Constanza—his mother—brought the beautifully carved cradle that he had slept in himself as a baby from her home tomorrow. It had been all he could do to dissuade her from visiting them tonight, such was her eagerness to see her grandson—but thankfully Leandro had been able to convince her that a visit was better left to the following day when Isabella and Raphael were more rested after their journey from London.

'You look a little tired. Why don't you come and make yourself at home?' he suggested, his deceptively cool gaze hiding the clamour of aroused senses inside him that were inevitably charged by the sight of Isabella's too-provoking beauty. Wearing a simple white linen shirt with light blue denim jeans and a black silver-buckled belt, her long ebony hair left unbounded and her feet fetchingly bare, she would have set the most impervious of male hearts to racing. If he were to point a film camera her way, Leandro had no doubt that that same captivating appeal would absolutely transfix an audience were she to appear on the screen. He knew his trade well enough to know that his instincts were right.

Studying her in silence as she moved across the room to seat herself on a couch draped with a vivid ochre-coloured Andalucian shawl, he could see why most people would naturally assume she was a true native of Spain—a bewitching *señorita* with eyes as black as treacle and a slow, sweet smile as sinful as *'Diablo'* himself.

'This is a great room,' she commented, her gaze contemplating her surroundings with seeming pleasure.

* * *

Where should she look first? Isabella's senses were confounded and captivated by the almost shockingly vivid colours that filled the room—colours that had no business complimenting each other but *did*. From the truly surprising candyfloss-pink-painted walls, to the mismatched rainbow hues on the chairs and couches and the breathlessly lovely interwoven Indian rugs that covered the generously proportioned stone-flagged floor. It was the unrestrained creation of an artist. Even if she never stepped outside the door and saw where they were, Isabella would instinctively know that she was under the spell of someone whose very soul was steeped in the culture and wilder landscapes of this arresting land. Even the books that crowded Leandro's bookcases had bright, unrestrained, eye-catching spines that made her long to go over and examine them more closely, to see what treasures the well-thumbed pages were hiding. The result of all this dramatic use of colour and material was a passionate, seductive sensibility that seemed to spill over into everything. It agitated Isabella's blood as well, making her acutely responsive to almost every single detail about this remarkable man at whose instigation she was here and whose steady commanding gaze drew her attention helplessly back to his as though magnetised.

'I am glad that you like it, Isabella. This is my favourite home and it is here that we will spend the majority of the time together.'

'Your favourite?' she queried.

'I have other homes in Pontevedra and in Paris where we will sometimes stay. But Madrid is my main base because I endeavour to arrange for most of my work to be here. I think it is important to help the economy by utilising local talent and locations whenever I can. Can I get you something to drink? Some wine, some juice, perhaps? We will eat later. In Madrid we are used to having dinner late…sometimes as late as eleven o'clock at night. Does that bother you?'

'Not at all. I ate on the plane and I'm not hungry anyway. I don't need a drink right now either, thanks.'

Mention of his work was enough to almost make Isabella beg him to tell her more. How she longed to have him talk freely to her about what inspired him, or moved him…what kind of scripts compelled him to direct them and what were his personal favourite films? Then, unwittingly catching the almost suggestive little smile curving his too disturbing mouth, she nervously recalled the fact that tonight she was expected to share a bed with this most enigmatic of men that the rest of the world seemed to hunger to know about. But as much as Isabella longed to know Leandro's loving again and had been craving his presence even more since giving birth to Raphael, she did not know if she was ready to be intimate with him. She was so confused. It still stung to remember that disparaging comment the woman at his offices had made about there always being some woman hanging onto his coat tails. Could she trust a man who seemed to treat relationships with women so lightly? He might be a good father to Raphael, but was he capable of being the kind of devoted husband that Isabella secretly dreamed of?

As if intuiting her thoughts, Leandro moved across

the room to stand before her. His gaze was quietly re-
flective as he stared down at her. 'You know that we are
sharing a room together tonight?' he commented.

All the hairs stood up on the back of Isabella's neck.
'I saw,' she replied quietly, her dark eyes widening. She
knew he wouldn't like what she had to say, but she *had*
to say it. 'To be honest…I don't really think that's such
a good idea.'

'Why not?' His eyes immediately blazed back his
irritation.

'Because a lot of time has passed since we were
together and I don't think I'm ready to jump straight
back into a physical relationship.'

'So what are you telling me, Isabella? That you
intend to live like a nun while we are together under the
same roof?' The twist of his lips was scornful.

'I need more time to…to think about that side of things.'

'*Dios!* Why are you being so deliberately difficult?' he flared.

Isabella flinched. 'I'm not being deliberately difficult!' she retaliated angrily. 'I did as you asked,
Leandro… I came to live here in Spain with you and our
baby! Isn't that enough change to be going on with for
the moment? My feelings are all churned up here! I
need time to deal with how I feel without you pressur-
ising me to sleep with you!'

'No!'

'What do you mean no?' Her heart was pounding in
her ears as Leandro reached out and locked his hand
round her wrist. His grip was like a tight iron band and,
before she could think what to do, he roughly pulled her

to her feet, his warm breath on her face. 'I have been aching to do this for ever and will not deny myself any longer,' he breathed huskily before bringing his lips down almost violently ardently upon Isabella's.

Yes, yes! Isabella cried silently as a jolt of pure lust streaked through her veins. *It's been too long…too long.* His at first coaxing, then demanding kiss was full of the vivacity and passion that sparked the creation of this boldly decorated room, and it was so hard to resist its rapture when she needed it more than she needed to take her next breath. Yet the possibility stole into her mind that Leandro might only be using her to gratify his own baser needs and the unwanted thought was like a snake in paradise. It kept pricking her consciousness like the sharpest pin and in the end she *had* to take action. Twisting her mouth away from his, Isabella leaned her elbows against his hard chest and broke free from his embrace. Her breath was ragged.

'I told you I needed time! Why won't you listen?'

Her dark eyes were full of tears and Leandro reeled from the wave of emotion and lust that swept through his body like a violent storm cloud and slowly drew the back of his hand across his mouth where her taste lingered like sensual sugar tempting and frustrating him. He knew from the way her body had trembled against his and the way she had moaned into his mouth that she welcomed his kisses, yet he could not understand why she held back from their ultimate union. He had already told her that he intended to marry her, so why was she so reticent? He wished she would be more honest with him because it immediately set up a feeling of mistrust inside him that she might have some other ulterior motive for keeping him out of her bed. Having experienced the manipulation and duplicity of women before, Leandro baulked at the idea of experiencing it again.

'I am listening, Isabella, but unfortunately you are not making any sense!' he said now. 'You have not been with anyone else since we were together, you tell me, *and* you have had my baby! It is clear that we have a strong connection between us, so what is the problem?'

How could she tell him that she was wary of his intentions because she didn't think he loved her? If the thought had not even crossed his mind, why would it mean anything to him if she voiced it? Swallowing back her tears, Isabella wearily pushed her fingers through her hair.

'I'm suddenly feeling quite tired. I think I'll go and lie down for a while.'

'That is your prerogative, of course, but do not think to divert the issue by doing so! I fully expect us to share a bed together tonight so you had better get used to the idea! While you are resting I intend to make some phone calls and catch up with some work. My housekeeper has left food in the kitchen for us when we are hungry so you must help yourself whenever that may be. Do not wait for me; I will see to myself when I am ready.' He paused, his glance hovering for a long unsettling moment on Isabella's mouth. 'The run of the house is yours. You must feel free to look around as much as you want to familiarise yourself where everything is. I will join you in our room later...that is a *promise*.' Leandro regretfully started to withdraw, feeling undeniable frustration that again there was such dissension between them. It did not bode well for the start of their renewed relationship.

'Leandro?'

'What is it?'

'What will I do tomorrow when you leave to go to work for the day?' Still smarting with indignation from his dictatorial attitude towards her, Isabella crossed her arms in front of her chest.

'You may do whatever you please, Isabella. Why not work on your book? There is of course a car at your disposal for when you want to go out…I will leave it out on the drive and the keys are on the dressing table in our room. There is also a map in the glove compartment so you cannot get lost. However, I would ask you to wait in a little while before you venture out because my mother, Constanza, is paying you and Raphael a visit first thing in the morning.'

'But you won't be here for her visit?' Feeling her heart accelerate a little in sudden panic at the idea of meeting his mother without him being present, Isabella anxiously stroked the delicate skin of her throat.

Shrugging, Leandro dropped his hands to his hips. 'I am sorry…but it is the first day of filming tomorrow and I have no idea what time I shall be home.' Reaching into the back pocket of his jeans, he took out his wallet and extracted some notes. 'Here is some money for you to get whatever you need for you and Raphael. Please take it…it is yours.'

'I don't want your money!'

Her dark eyes flared because Isabella was genuinely embarrassed that Leandro should give her money…as if she were some kind of pauper. She might not be exactly rich but she had not come to Spain without any funds whatsoever! His answering scowl was immediate and foreboding. 'Isabella,' he intoned seriously, 'you are the mother of my son and soon to be my wife. Do not act as if I am treating you like some charity case. From now on my money is yours too and both you and our son must have whatever you need without question. Is that clear?'

'Leandro,' she replied a little breathlessly, ignoring the money in his outstretched hand, 'it is far too early to talk of financial arrangements when there is still so much to sort out. And marriage is something that we have yet to properly discuss too.'

'*Bastante!* Enough! It has been a long day, no? And perhaps something of a strain for both of us.' He put the money down on a chair behind him and sighed. 'Now is not the time for us to argue over the matter. Go and take your rest and I will be in my office.'

And before Isabella could even *think* of pressing the point, Leandro made his absence in the room acutely felt as he abruptly vacated it.

Checking on Raphael for the umpteenth time since she'd returned to their room, Isabella saw with deeply maternal satisfaction that her little boy continued to sleep peacefully in his travel cot by the side of the bed. Picking up the novel she'd been reading, she straightened her bookmark and closed it. Instead of reading, she leant back against the plumped up pillows covered in scented, immaculate white linen and released a sigh that seemed to emanate from her soul. It was almost half past midnight and there was still neither sight nor sound of Leandro. Isabella's sigh helplessly transmuted into a yawn. It *had* been a long day and she had no idea how much longer it would be before Leandro joined her in bed. In spite of her previous outburst about needing more time to assimilate her feelings, the thought of his presence caused a frisson of passionate longing to bolt through her bloodstream and she suddenly wished with all her heart that he didn't have to desert her tomorrow and go to work.

And how was she going to handle meeting his mother when he wasn't there? What must be going through the woman's mind at the thought of meeting Isabella for the first time? The woman who had given birth to her son's child? The woman whom her son now declared he was going to *marry*?

Feeling slightly dizzy at the mere idea of becoming Mrs Leandro Reyes, Isabella put away her book, levelled the pillow behind her head and switched out the small brass lamp with its exotic beaded hem that was glowing beside her. As the restful silence in the room reached out to her and she was cocooned in darkness she determinedly closed her eyes—only to open them again a minute later when an insistent vision of her beloved grandfather floated into her mind. He'd been shaking his head and asking wisely, 'Do you really love him, Isabella? And does he love you?'

'Yes, Grandfather,' Isabella whispered in the dark as she pulled the quilt up to her chin, 'I *do* love him…but I won't marry him unless I am certain that he loves me…'

* * *

A stream of phone calls demanding his attention with a seemingly never-ending list of work-related problems to untangle before filming started the following morning, Leandro regretfully never made it back to his bed that night. Instead, as the dawn started to chase away the darkness outside his study window he crossed the room to the colourful couch strewn with cushions that he often utilised when he was working late and shut his eyes for just forty minutes before rising again and going in search of a shower.

When he quietly entered the bedroom and crept over to Isabella's side of the bed to gaze down at his sleeping son in his travel cot, he was filled with such a torrent of love and emotion that even though his eyes burned from lack of sleep he could have stayed just watching Raphael slumber until he woke.

Silently cursing the timing of this new film he was going to direct—when for the first time in his illustrious career he would have preferred to do something he considered *far* more important—Leandro turned his attention to Isabella. Like their son, she lay fast asleep, her dark hair spread out in silken disarray upon the contrasting white pillow, one arm beneath her and the other flung out on top of the lilac-coloured silk of the eiderdown. Her arms were slender and as elegant as a porcelain ballerina's and, seeing the soft rise and fall of her breasts beneath her white gown, Leandro experienced an almost painful urge to get in beside her and wake her in the most sensually loving way he could think of. The row they had had played on his mind and his need to make up with her in the one way that would knock down all barriers between them was almost overwhelming.

Biting back his frustration at knowing that that was not immediately possible, he left the room for the adjoining bathroom and, when the door was firmly shut behind him, could not help emitting a gravel-voiced groan at the incessant and insistent ache that had gripped the most personal and vital part of his anatomy in a most passionate vice. Somehow, he would have to wait until tomorrow.

Isabella had been kissed soundly several times and hugged fiercely within an inch of her life by Constanza Reyes...but that was nothing compared to the shower of love and delight poured down upon an initially wary, then later happily smiling Raphael. Her little son seemed to take equal felicity and pleasure in the effusive attentions of the extraordinarily attractive yet undoubtedly maternal brunette that was Leandro's mother— and, therefore, his grandmother.

As Isabella rather self-consciously tried to familiarise herself with the large and well-appointed kitchen, endeavouring to make tea for Constanza and herself as well as mash up some banana for Raphael's breakfast, the older woman kept up a stream of unrelenting chatter with the beguiled infant who sat in her lap and just basked in all the attention as though it were simply ordained.

'He is beautiful...beautiful just like his father, *sí*?' Glancing up at Isabella as she stirred the leaves in the teapot before replacing the yellow pottery lid, Constanza beamed happily at the younger woman.

Afraid that Leandro's mother might have some awkward questions about Isabella proving validity of her claim that Raphael was indeed the progeny of her only son, she had been so relieved when he had been accepted from practically the moment she saw him. It was, of course, his unusual coloured eyes that had answered any doubts she might have had. If they had been the more common brown, blue, green or hazel of most of the population, then there might well have been some awkward questions and, understandably, even suspicions. But already Constanza had affirmed that Raphael was the mirror of his father at the same age and her delight in them both was a joy to be witnessed.

'*Sí*...I mean, yes...he is beautiful like his father.'

Isabella had no hesitation in admitting the truth. Even though she'd been troubled that Leandro had *not* joined her in bed last night when he had sworn to do just that, and thinking that maybe her earlier anger had made him stay away, she understood that because of the nature of his work, and in particular the timing involved in making a film, right now it demanded his attention before anything else. She told herself she would just have to get used to the idea... That was, if things between them became more amicable and she decided to stay for good. Her stomach tensing at the unknowable nature of her future as far as her relationship with Leandro was concerned, Isabella brought the tea over to the table, then returned to the spotlessly clean counter to fetch the little bowl of mashed banana for her son.

'You cannot know what this little one's existence

means to me, Isabella,' Constanza said in earnest, her hand covering the younger woman's as she sat down opposite her. 'Seventeen months ago my husband was killed crossing a road by a crazy drunk driver and my heart was as heavy as the cold marble headstone that sits in front of his grave. I did not know how I should go on living.' Shaking her head, she sighed softly, garnering her courage, then bent and kissed the top of Raphael's curly dark hair. 'When Leandro rang me to tell me of his unbelievable news…it was as though God had heard my prayers and given me the one thing that would ease my hurt beyond all others. Thank you, Isabella…*thank you* for having this beautiful child and helping me find a reason to go on.'

Blinking back the scalding tears that were suddenly awash in her eyes, Isabella simply stared at Constanza and allowed her hand to be held. She remembered the haunting shadow of pain that had crossed Leandro's face when he'd told her the news and a wave of sorrow washed over her. Her heart swelled with renewed love for him, but she also experienced deep grief that he'd clearly not wanted her sympathy or her comfort. Now a new resolve infiltrated her bones. When he came home that night, Isabella was determined that they would talk. She could simply not let one more day disappear into another without speaking frankly and full-heartedly.

'My baby gives me a reason for living too, Constanza,' she confessed softly, smiling first at her son, then at the other woman with unreserved warmth, silently wishing that her own mother could be even half as appreciative and understanding…

* * *

Leandro did not return to the farmhouse until after nine in the evening. Raphael was already fast asleep in the exquisite antique cradle that Constanza had so lovingly given him and Isabella had eaten her share of the wonderful paella that his housekeeper had left for them both…alone. Her body clock had yet to adjust to the later eating habits of most of the local population. She'd been sitting with her legs curled up beneath her on the sofa, trying to concentrate on brushing up on her extremely inadequate Spanish from the dictionary that she'd found on one of the bookshelves, when she heard the tyres of Leandro's car crunch onto the gravel drive. Since her grandfather had died, Isabella had had little opportunity to enlarge upon the vocabulary he had taught her, and now she regretted not doing a language class to improve her woeful lack of skill in that area. It seemed even more important now because of her son's father's heritage. Hearing a door slam, she put the book to one side and swung her legs onto the floor. She was hastily getting to her feet when Leandro opened the door and strode into the room.

'*Hola!*' Naturally using the Spanish greeting for 'hello' instead of English, Leandro ambushed her senses with the most devastating grin that would have melted chilled butter straight from the refrigerator and for a moment stopped all sensible thought in its tracks. In fact, Isabella found herself so flustered that she suddenly felt extremely awkward replying to his greeting in the same vein—even though she desperately wanted to show him how willing she was to learn the language and use it.

'Hi. How did your day go?'

'It is improving every second now that I am home and gazing at you,' he answered without hesitation. But even as his provocative teasing made her shiver with secret delighted pleasure Isabella straight away recognised the evidence of tiredness and strain that was etched into the riveting contours of his handsome face. Shrugging off his leather jacket, he discarded it onto a chair and came towards her. Isabella could swear that she heard her own heart beating in her ears as he approached across the exotic Indian rug at her feet. 'I regret that I did not fulfil my promise of joining you in our bed last night,' he told her, his haunting glance holding her captivated, 'but perhaps you were secretly pleased that I did not?'

Her heart aching that he might seriously think so, Isabella touched his sleeve. 'You're wrong. I did miss you.'

Studying her hard for a moment, as if he needed to make sure she was telling him the truth, he swallowed and looked relieved.

'I did not make it because inevitably before shooting a film there are always last-minute problems that need sorting out. I spent most of the night talking on the telephone and had a short siesta before I left, on the couch in my study. I did not want to risk disturbing you and Raphael when you were both fast asleep. Now tell me…how did you spend *your* day, Isabella?'

Studying her lips with a wave of lustful need suddenly stampeding hotly through his blood, Leandro waited with barely disguised impatience for her to speak. To hear her confess that she had missed him last night in their bed was more than gratifying. All day, work had inevitably demanded his full, unpreoccupied attention, but as soon as shooting had finished and the film crew had started to pack up prior to leaving for the night Leandro's thoughts had naturally broken free of the requirements of his job and gravitated to his newly acquired family instead. Now as the intoxicating scent of woman and heat entrapped him, he could think of at least a dozen ways how Isabella could help him throw off the tensions of the day.

'Your mother came to visit us this morning and she stayed until lunchtime. She was wonderful with Raphael… I liked her a lot,' Isabella told him eagerly.

'She rang me to tell me. Apart from going crazy over her grandson, she had some very complimentary things to say about you too, Isabella.'

'Constanza is very easy to like, Leandro. She was very warm and kind and we talked about lots of things.'

'Oh… Such as?'

'You as a little boy…the mischief you got up to.' She tried to coax a smile from him but he was suddenly wearing that wary look he adopted some-times. Isabella decided not to let it curtail what she had been going to say. She desperately wanted to have a frank discussion with him.

'Anything else?' he asked.

'Yes…we talked a little about your father.'

'Really?' The flash of pain and anger in his piercing gaze riveted Isabella to the floor.

CHAPTER NINE

'YES, really. Leandro, are we going to avoid speaking about your father like this for ever?' Isabella's mouth turned dry as she gave voice to her frustration and anguish. 'He was obviously a hugely important part of your life and I can see that you're still hurting over his death. If you'd just talk to me about it I know that I could help—'

'I will deal with it in my own way—the way I have been doing for the past seventeen months. I do not need anybody's help!'

The discernible flash of agony in Leandro's face was mutual agony for Isabella to witness. Now she wished she'd bided her time before bringing the subject up, but at the same time couldn't see how they could avoid mentioning it when his mother had so heart-rendingly brought it to Isabella's attention earlier on in the day.

'So you're going to shut me out? Not even let me help comfort you?'

'My mother should not have talked to you about him.'

'Why not? If she could trust me, why can't you, Leandro?'

The expression in his eyes pierced Isabella's heart.

'Because I cannot! That is why!'

Isabella flinched at the sting of rage in his voice. 'All right. I can see that you're not ready to talk about this so I'll drop the subject…for now.'

'How is Raphael? I know he must be asleep, but I want to go and see him.'

Already on his way to the door, Leandro paused almost reluctantly to hear Isabella's reply. He seemed eager to get away from her, in fact. Hurt that he obviously did not have enough trust in her yet to share his feelings about the terrible tragedy that had befallen him and his loved ones, yet determined to get through to him somehow, Isabella swallowed down the nugget of pain as though a bitter pill and also moved towards the door. 'I'll come with you.'

'No.' His arresting grey eyes glinted with disapproval. 'I would like to spend some time with my son, alone. Perhaps you would open a bottle of wine and pour us both a glass for when I return?'

Hardly knowing how to deal with the profuse sense of rejection that throbbed harshly through her bloodstream, Isabella shrugged and smoothed her hand awkwardly down over her hip. 'All right. I'll see you in a little while, then.'

As he sat on the edge of the bed and examined the peaceful sleeping figure of his little son in the familiar, intricately carved mahogany cradle that was a proud family heirloom Leandro dropped his head into his hands and finally surrendered to the floodgates of emotion that had been threatening to burst open all day.

Unable to halt the flow of tears that washed into his eyes, he simply let them fall—his heart so full that words would not have been possible even if they were demanded of him right then. If only his father were still alive and could see the perfect little infant so restfully slumbering in the Reyes family cradle! He missed the steady, unwavering love that had allowed him to just be himself without judgement and he yearned to experience the monumental bear hugs again that Leandro was certain could crush a less strong man. The joy and pride in Vincente's still-handsome lined face when his son had been accorded acclaim and admiration for his work and the wise and thoughtful advice that had often been a refuge for Leandro when all other solutions to a problem had failed, were like missing parts of his own body...

But losing his father and his best friend was worse than losing a limb, in his opinion. Even a limb could be replaced with an artificial one and a person could still function...could still *heal*. He didn't know if he would ever come to terms with the abrupt parting from the man who had raised him. It was funny...but sometimes a man did not know what he *did* want until he had to do without something, he considered. Now he wanted to be able to present Vincente with his grandchild but that would never, ever be possible.

'You will regret it if you never have children,' his father had counselled him sagely too many times for him to remember. 'It is not now that you will feel it...but *later* when you get older.'

Shaking his head, Leandro raised it once again to gaze upon his beautiful little boy's sleeping form and, apart from the fierce paternal love that seemed to flow into every cell in his body, he was filled with a stunning profound consolation. He might not ever be able to lessen the pain of his father's loss—but he was not without consolation. Suddenly aware that the heavens had accorded him the most amazing gift of all by giving him a son—a son he had not even known lived until he'd gone to London a few days ago— Leandro let the realisation sink deep inside him. Scrubbing at the moisture that had trickled down onto his beard-roughened jaw, he stretched out a hand to tenderly touch his fingertips to Raphael's soft pinked cheek. The sorrow that had brought him to tears only moments ago was fervently replaced by the most intoxicating elation.

This child was his...created by the love he had made to Isabella...the bewitching and sensitive woman who had blown through his defences like a small cyclone. Could he learn to trust her with his feelings even a little? It seemed like a very tall order right now when his emotions were still so raw. Leandro had long since forgiven the woman who had cheated on him, but the betrayal by someone he'd dared to let into his heart had honestly felt as though it had scarred him for life. How could he be sure that Isabella would not do the same thing? It would be worse...far worse than before because they had a son together... The only way to let her know that he absolutely commanded her loyalty and commitment was to make her his wife... The sooner they could arrange it, the better.

* * *

Crossing the stone-flagged floor in his bare feet, Leandro glanced at Isabella—seemingly engrossed in her book as she sat back on the couch with her legs drawn up beside her. Smiling enigmatically, he slid a CD out of its cover and slipped it onto the player that was situated in the middle of a large bookcase. As the passionate sounds of flamenco cut a gut-wrenching, startled swathe through the silence he moved across to the heavy oak coffee-table where the glass of red wine that he'd asked Isabella to pour for him invitingly beckoned. But instead of reaching for it he reached instead for Isabella's hand. Smiling deeply into her eyes, he commanded throatily, 'Dance with me.'

She was so astonished by this surprising request, there was simply no time to think of refusing as Isabella felt herself compelled to her feet. In less than a heartbeat she was in Leandro's arms, the innate sense of man and muscle and warm, silky skin sending an avalanche of superlative sensation pulsating throughout her entire being. As he led her round the room, clasping her to him with a firm, assured hand—her body helplessly moving to the fascinating rhythm of his—he stayed silent, seemingly lost in the rousing sensual sounds of Spanish guitar that seduced the very air around them with ravishing intent. Isabella hardly dared breathe. But after another minute or two Leandro brushed his lips tantalisingly against her ear and said, 'It feels so good to have you in my arms again, Isabella. They have been empty without you.'

Casting aside very real fears that there had been other women occupying that place in his arms during the past eighteen months when she hadn't been in his life,

Isabella couldn't help but wish that he truly meant the too-beguiling comment. 'That night in the Port of Vigo seems a long time ago now,' she replied softly.

He stopped moving round the floor with her to the music and, setting her only slightly apart from him, stroked her long hair back from either side of her face to more closely engage her attention. '*Sí...too* long,' he agreed enigmatically with a little half-smile. 'And so much has happened since that unforgettable night. I have not yet asked you how you felt when you learned that you were expecting my child?'

There it was again...that almost fierce stamp of possession in his tone that had both confused and elated Isabella from the very beginning. Heat poured through her like a honeyed potion, relaxing every muscle yet at the same time making her shiver with longing. Did she ever dare tell Leandro that her heart had leapt like crazy at the idea of having his child? How would he take such a declaration?

'Like you...I was stunned that such a thing had happened...but, after getting over the shock, I was determined to keep my baby,' she told him honestly, her dark eyes glowing deeper black, 'no matter what happened.' She honestly hadn't at any point considered having a termination. The very idea elicited chills of horror. Isabella saw the answering gleam of satisfaction in Leandro's examining hypnotic gaze.

'*Sí*...you kept our baby and for that I am eternally grateful to you, Isabella. Especially as it must have made life quite difficult for you, no?'

'I don't regret a moment. Raphael is everything to me.'

'I can see that. And now…he is everything to me too. You understand that is why I wanted you both to come to Madrid? Why I could not wait?'

'I understand. But there is still a lot to resolve, Leandro. We can't automatically assume that this will be a permanent arrangement.'

'Yes, we can! I will make you my wife, Isabella!' he insisted firmly, his hands cupping her hips and forcibly moving her body more intimately against his.

'Marriage is not a thing that should be decided so suddenly,' Isabella asserted, even stronger shivers assailing her as Leandro swept her with a distinctly devouring glance.

'It is only sudden because of the circumstances we find ourselves in, no? And that does not mean it is wrong. I only know that we both want the best thing for our son and that is ultimately why we must be together.' He lightly touched her face with the palm of his hand. 'It will not be so bad being married to me, will it?'

It would be heaven…if he only said that he loved her too. Isabella tried to dismiss the doubt that filled her mind and cling to a more positive hope. Maybe Leandro would grow to love her in time? Maybe even learn to trust her? But then again…what if he didn't? What if one day he met somebody and *really* fell in love? Might he not then feel trapped by his marriage to Isabella…trapped by the fact that he had a child to support? Determinedly, she endeavoured to put aside her distress. When she was alone again, there would be plenty of time to call upon deeper introspection and make clearer decisions.

'By the way,' Leandro remarked, 'I made a few enquiries today about your letters and phone calls that I did not get. It will not surprise you to learn that everyone is denying all knowledge of ever having received them, but do not be concerned. I am quite well aware that they do not want to incur my wrath. I am furious, of course, and it is frustrating for me too, but I also realise that there is little I can do now except try to mend the wrong that was done to both of us. At least I have my son now…so let us not think any more on problems. Do you agree? My day at work has had enough tension in it to make me just want to forget everything but you and Raphael and just relax. The flamenco gets into your blood, does it not?'

It did…*he* did.

Grateful that Leandro had unequivocally believed her efforts to get in touch with him—despite what his 'people' were saying—Isabella determined to let the matter rest. Right now she was simply too overcome by the man's too-alluring charms to let herself be pulled down by regret and despondency. It was a delirious and heady combination…Leandro *and* the flamenco.

'We are going to go out tonight to have some tapas,' he told her, smiling as he started to dance with her again. 'My mother should be here in a while to stay and watch over Raphael for us. I want to show you Madrid at night and have you to myself for a while.'

'Oh? Constanza never mentioned it to me that you'd asked her to baby-sit.' The idea of going out with Leandro and seeing Madrid with him by night was admittedly exciting, but Isabella was also a little put out that she had not figured in the equation when it came to making such an arrangement with his mother. Not that she didn't trust Constanza—she was lovely and Isabella had no worries about her ability to take care of Raphael—but even so…

'Isabella.' Once more coming to a halt, Leandro studied her in all seriousness, a deep furrow of concern between his dark brows. 'If we are to become close—as I fully intend us to be for Raphael's sake—I want to spend some private time with you, getting to know you. Is that something to be suspicious of? My mother already adores her grandchild—I can assure you that she will probably sit by his bedside right up until we come home again and she will think herself in paradise!'

Feeling her face burn beneath his intensely disturbing gaze, Isabella shrugged awkwardly, exceedingly conscious that the pads of his thumbs were stroking back and forth across her palms with the kind of sensual dexterity that made her want to either plead for mercy or beg for more of the same. 'But won't you be tired? I mean…you have to get up early for work tomorrow, don't you?'

He laughed and, along with the near orgasmic sensations he was already producing in her with his thumbs, the sound made her legs turn to jelly.

'*Madrileños* are notorious for getting by on very little sleep, Isabella, as you will soon learn. We still rise early but we lunch and have dinner late, and if we go out to a bar or a nightclub we can be out until three or four in the morning until returning home again. However, I promise I will get you home at a reasonable hour tonight. I know you will be anxious to get back to

Raphael and also…tonight I will *definitely* be sharing our bed with you, Isabella.'

Lifting her hand to his lips, Leandro grazed her fingertips and held her gaze for long, trembling seconds before releasing it again. By the time he had done with her, Isabella wondered how on earth she hadn't just simply melted into a limpid pool of helpless delight on the floor.

'Tell me about your grandfather…this "Raphael Morentes"?'

They were tucked away in a corner booth of a busy, noisy, but infectiously appealing tapas bar with its flamenco music filling the air—and full to the brim with stylish young *Madrileños* clearly enjoying themselves. Leandro's shoulder pressed up disturbingly close to Isabella's as he smilingly focused all his attention on her. Sipping a little Rioja wine before answering him, Isabella tried not to be too dazzled by those incredible quicksilver eyes of his—but, quite frankly, this was one topic of conversation that she had no trouble indulging in.

'He was just the best…a kind, gentle, loving man. He came to England when my father died and bought a house near where my mother lived so that he could be close to us and help take care of us. Can you imagine what that must have taken for him to do such a thing? To leave his small village in rural Spain and immerse himself in life in London? Anyway…I was only two at the time and I have no real memory of my father. But he was my grandfather's only son and he was heartbroken when he lost him. I suppose he transferred all his love and attention onto me then…and even when my mother remarried, he continued to help take care of me.'

She swallowed hard across the painful ache of emotion inside her throat that the memory inevitably instigated. Contemplating her sorrow, Leandro was watchful but silent. Isabella gave him an apologetic smile. 'I'm sorry…I still get a bit choked up when I talk about him. He died when I was twenty-one and even though that's quite a few years ago now…I still find it hard to accept that he's not here any more.'

'*Sí*…I understand.' He clasped her hand and wove his fingers through hers. The unexpected contact made Isabella catch her breath, as did the undisputed warmth that she was receiving from his sympathetic glance. 'He sounds like a man whose company I would very much have enjoyed.'

'Oh, you would have!' Her pleasure at the thought helplessly spilled out and her dark eyes sparkled like newly polished crystal. 'Like you, he loved music and art and stories and philosophy and he was so wise. He saw every problem as a gift…something given to us to help strengthen our character and to better understand ourselves, and the world. That's why I wanted to walk the Camino… He always talked about it like it was some kind of a quest. Shades of King Arthur and the Knights of the Round Table, I suppose.' She grinned. 'That's why I always felt it was something I *had* to do.'

'And you did it. Your grandfather would have been proud of you, Isabella.' Locking his fingers even tighter through hers, Leandro surprised her by touching his lips to the side of her mouth, his unshaven jaw slightly rough against her own softer textures, his riveting warmth and the spicy sensual stamp of his cologne guaranteeing that she was duly mesmerised by him…as usual. Just as he pulled away, the shocking flare of a camera flash went off in their faces.

'*Imbécil!*'

As the almost-blinding effect of the flash subsided Leandro rose angrily to his feet to address the grinning young man with shaved head and a piercing in one eyebrow who had been so bold as to steal a picture. The camera he held in his hands was clearly a professional one used by members of the paparazzi, and as heads turned to survey the scene Leandro let loose a torrent of Spanish invective and looked about to grab the man by the scruff of his shirt until the photographer suddenly turned and fled through the crowd. Another man emerged from the interested throng who'd viewed the incident and shouted something out to Leandro. Seeing him nod his acquiescence to whatever he had been proposing, Isabella was not surprised to see the second man chase off in the same direction as the other one.

He told himself he should be used to this. It was not always possible to maintain his privacy to the zealously guarded degree he might wish—but still Leandro was shocked and furious at the unacceptable intrusion to his and Isabella's evening. With his heart still pounding, his jaw was clenched in agitation as he sat down again next to her. 'I doubt if my friend Pepe will catch up to him now, so no doubt we can expect a picture in the morning papers. *Maldita sea!* I am sorry that you had to witness that, Isabella. Most people leave me alone in my own town, but the news of me making a new film has obviously leaked out and the paparazzi must have been hoping for just such an opportunity as I gave them tonight. Come…I am afraid we must find another place less popular to enjoy our tapas this evening.'

'We don't have to go anywhere else if you'd rather just go straight home.' Instinctively Isabella touched his arm, her expression concerned.

'I have to live my life, Isabella, and so do you. It is my wish that you see some of the city that I love tonight…enjoy some of the food and listen to the music. There is no reason we should hurry back home simply because a paparazzo flashed a camera in our faces! Whoever he is, he has his picture and won't come looking for us again tonight. If he does…then I will handle it…*sí*?'

'All right.' Quelling her disquiet, Isabella accepted the hand that Leandro held out to her as he stood up. 'Whatever you think is best.'

CHAPTER TEN

CONSTANZA had retired to her bed and, when Leandro went to check, he had discovered that his mother had moved Raphael's cradle in with her for the night. Torn between wanting her son back by her side as well as seeing the practicality of the action Constanza had taken, Isabella moved distractedly across the living room to the over-stacked bookcase that was always going to be the most irresistible draw for her. Trying to quell the unsettled feeling that seemed to have infiltrated her bones, she thought over the wonderful evening she had just spent in Leandro's charismatic company. He had soon put aside his irritation at that photographer taking their picture and had become irresistibly warm and attentive throughout the rest of the evening together. They had shared food, dancing and laughter, but Isabella couldn't help noticing that he was still reluctant to reveal anything too personal about his life and work. He certainly had not felt sufficiently compelled to even mention his father to her.

His reticence definitely bothered Isabella when she had willingly shared with him how much she had loved her grandfather, and how she still missed him to this day. Now, because of his lack of trust, she had this unshakeable notion that Leandro somehow expected her to disappoint him and, if that was the case, how was Isabella supposed to disprove him if he would never really let his guard down and share his true feelings with her? To her alarm, tears blurred and stung her gaze as she picked up a book on Andalucia and started to haphazardly flick through it.

'Isabella?'

She sucked in a steadying breath at the sound of her name and turned around slowly. Leandro was standing in the centre of the room with his hands on his lean, narrow hips and even though her vision was disturbed by her tears Isabella could easily see the longing in his expression—in spite of the distance between them. A bittersweet, answering need shot through her insides almost violently.

'Yes?'

'It is time for bed.' Glancing down at his wristwatch, he dispatched a rueful yet mesmerising grin that unsteadied her even more. 'It is nearly a quarter to two in the morning and I have to rise at six to go to work.'

'You go ahead… I'm not tired yet.' Turning deliberately back to the bookshelf, Isabella returned the book she was holding to the slot that had housed it. Sensing a barefooted Leandro walk slowly up behind her, she harshly willed her treacherous tears away. He already had enough of an advantage over her when she loved him with all her heart and he clearly did not trust her enough to return the feeling. She had to be *strong*, she reminded herself…not let him see what he could easily reduce her to. Trust and love were everything. Isabella had learned that from her grandfather.

'I did not necessarily mean that we had to go straight to sleep, Isabella.' Nuzzling her neck with his too tempting warm mouth, Leandro slipped his arms around her waist in the jade linen shift dress she'd worn for their evening out together. Suffused by irresistible need that only a stone statue would have been able to ignore—and Isabella definitely *wasn't* made out of stone—she acknowledged her quickening breath and trembling limbs in silent acquiescence, even if her reaction was entwined with heartbreak as well as desire. 'What do you want of me, Leandro?'

He knew by her tone that she kept a part of herself back from him and, though it conflicted with his undeniable need for physical contact—soft and slightly breathless—her sweet voice whispered across Leandro's nerve endings like the most sensuous invitation. His body had been so aware of her all evening that it was in a state of permanent erotic tension. Now that tension beseeched him for some release. He lifted her hair and kissed the back of her neck. As he did so he reached for the zipper of her dress and slowly tugged it down. The sight of her beautiful naked back pushed Leandro's already inflamed desire up a heated notch. He moved his hands either side of her sexy womanly hips, the kind he had a very strong penchant for, and brought her body into almost painful contact with his. He felt himself tense with insatiable hunger. With her firm satin skin and her very touchable shapely behind, Isabella was a woman who would stoke the fires of passion even in a eunuch. And she had had *his* baby… That fact alone surely denoted that she was *his* and nobody else's?

Experiencing an undeniable burn of jealousy at the idea that another man might lust after her, or give her body pleasure, Leandro knew a sudden dominant need to stake his claim on Isabella. Easily unhooking the back of her silky black bra, he moved his hands possessively either side of her body to cup her breasts. *Dios mio!* They were definitely fuller and sexier since she had had Raphael and her nipples tightened provocatively the moment they came into contact with his flesh, the puckered velvet tips responding even more fervently when Leandro squeezed them. The roar in his blood made him shut his eyes to absorb the incredible wave of torrid sensation that seized his body and he ground his pelvis up against Isabella's irresistible bottom and sensed his arousal harden like steel. The need for sleep was far from his mind when he thought about having to get up early to start filming in the morning… Right now he seemed to be surviving on pure adrenaline alone. But sleep deprivation aside—he would happily forgo any number of sleepless nights to make love with this woman.

'*This* is what I want, Isabella,' he breathed next to her shoulder blade as she arched her back to allow his hands even better access to her breasts. As her long hair brushed the side of his cheekbone and the intoxicating scent of jasmine slammed powerfully into his already seduced senses, Leandro expelled a harsh, rasping groan and moved his hands down her back onto her bottom. Sliding his palm onto the deliciously satin-textured skin beneath her skimpy underwear, he almost forgot to breathe as his fingers dipped lower and made an exquisitely arresting foray between her slender thighs.

'I want more of this impossible *wild* need that seems to consume me whenever I am near you.' He pushed his finger fully into her scalding heat and at her long breathless gasp felt his erection strain almost torturously against the zip of his fly. 'I want to be inside you, Isabella… I want us to forget the world, forget *everything*, I want to make you forget your own name as I push you to the edge of need…as you are pushing me to the edge of need right now.' When he added another finger and pressed a little higher and deeper, Leandro experienced for himself the shock waves of pleasure that rocked Isabella's aroused body and he stayed with her, whispering and coaxing her uninhibited response as she allowed him to help her make that final journey into bliss. Shaking, she turned slowly round to face him. Aching with an ache beyond measure to pull her into his arms and kiss her…instead of fulfilling his desire, Leandro stayed exactly where he was. His whole body was screaming for release too, but some greater instinct made him hold back. With her jade dress half on and half off, her rich dark eyes glazed with the stunned passion he had helped bring to fruition, Isabella regarded him for long, disquieting seconds before speaking. For some reason, Leandro's heart began to thump unevenly.

Gazing into his sculpted handsome features, the dark, perpetually tousled silky hair, and the tormenting mercurial glance that had consumed her with such delight and desire from the very beginning, Isabella could not hold back what her heart ached so profoundly to say. She had not walked the Camino to hide in a corner any more, or to play second fiddle to somebody else's desires or not say what she wanted. She wanted this man… She wanted his undying love and commitment to her and Raphael. More than anything, she wanted his *trust* and for him to know that she would never betray him either in deed or word. If she couldn't have that, then she didn't know if she could endure being with him day after day and feeling that he shut an important part of himself away from her.

'What is it, Isabella? Is something wrong?'

Swallowing across the knot of anxiety in her throat, Isabella shook her head and as she did so dragged up the sleeves of her dress so that the garment covered her once more. 'I love you, Leandro… I know you might not want to hear that right now…but it's the truth. The thing is…I'm still confused about how you feel about me and I need to know. Will you tell me?'

Her question imploded inside Leandro like a tiny but lethal incendiary. Where she was concerned, he definitely harboured the strongest, almost overpowering attraction and she had had his baby…his *son*. For that reason alone, Leandro would always hold Isabella in the highest regard and esteem. In all likelihood, he would grow to care for her even more when she became his wife. Yet he could not answer in all honesty that he loved her. That was a commitment that he was still too wary to surrender to, even though during the past eighteen months she had dominated his thinking too often for his peace of mind. So much so that he been driven to find her again. Catching her hand in his, Leandro turned it over and back again in the nest of his palm, examining the slender, light weight of it with undoubted pleasure even as his blood thrummed with faint apprehension. Raising his gaze, he met her troubled frown with a deliberately flirtatious smile.

'I feel many good things about you, Isabella. We can be good together, *sí*? I sensed that from the first time we met. Why else would I seek you out again after all this time? And that was *before* I even knew or dreamed that you had had my baby. You are a most beguiling and beautiful woman and clearly a wonderful mother to Raphael...and I will give you my promise to be the best husband I can be to you... You will not regret our marriage.'

So...he could not tell her that he loved her? It was just as Isabella had suspected it might be. She would have tugged her hand free from his if he had not held onto it with such an iron grip. Meeting his gaze—the blistering need reflected there cutting her to the quick—Isabella decided not to withdraw in haste or hurt. Instead of making a scene, she would give him what he wanted...what they *both* wanted...and afterwards she would just have to regroup and garner all the inner strength she could summon to withstand the knowledge. But she wasn't ready to give up on Leandro's love yet. Somehow she would find a way to reach him.

Raising her hand, she touched his face, the scratchy stubble on his hard, unshaven jaw infused with the se-

ductive heat from his body. Swallowing down her hurt,
she let the intimate contact with him infuse her with
carnal sensation instead—knowing that on this level at
least she *could* claim some devotion from him…

'Didn't you say something about wanting to be
inside me?' she asked, her voice lowered to an invitingly soft whisper.

'*Dios!*' His mouth met hers in a hard, hot exploration, his rough jaw unforgiving against Isabella's infinitely smoother and softer skin. When he lifted his head
after a while, his breath came in short, sharp bursts and
his grey eyes were wild with fierce desire. 'Nothing
and *no one* is going to keep me from sharing a bed with
you tonight, Isabella!'

Lifting her into his arms, his iron strength support-
ing her body as though its weight were entirely insignificant, he headed down the corridors of the beautiful
finca to their bedroom…

Her hands curled around the brass rungs of the bedstead
as his mouth aroused such heavenly sensations inside
her that Isabella had barely guessed existed. In bed he
had most definitely become that disreputable, irresistible pirate who'd taunted her from the beginning when
he'd told her that he would *ravish* her if she wished him
to. Now, lifting his head from where he'd been licking
with his velvet tongue, causing the sweetest, most erotic
devastation known to woman, there was a challenging,
almost demanding glint in his eye. His hands almost
roughly pushing her thighs apart, he raised himself up
and pushed inside her. His hard satin heat made Isabella

moan out loud, her hands releasing from their grip on the brass rungs of the bedstead to push through the silken strands of Leandro's tousled hair instead as his thrusts into her body became more and more focused and possessive...until finally, he cried out with the violence of his release. His hands on Isabella's breasts, he lay his head between them and the slick sweat on his body adhered stickily to hers, the soft musk scent of their loving filling her nostrils. She had never felt so complete or connected to another human being with such soul-deep intensity. In her arms, Leandro *did* need her and, even though he might fight against falling in love with her, Isabella hoped and prayed that that just *might* become a battle he would lose... Inadvertently, her eyes filled with tears.

Leandro felt the brief but distinct shiver that went through Isabella's body. His eyes drooping with exhaustion and replete from their passionate, uninhibited lovemaking, he almost did not want to speak. All he wanted to do was lie here in her arms, closer than close with her body and her touch, his senses entrapped by the bewitching erotic spell she had cast over him and praying never to be free from it. With an effort, he raised his head to smile at her. He heard the audible yet quiet sigh of resignation that emitted from her breath.

'What is it? Am I hurting you? Do you want me to move?'

'No...it's not that.' Her dark eyes swam into his and Leandro felt his own breath hitch. She resembled a dark misty-eyed angel who had seen the desperate travails of

humans firsthand and had her heart broken as a conse-
quence. In spite of his concern for what might be the
cause of her sadness, Leandro sensed his blood heat
with almost violent longing at the sight of her.

'When I left your friend's hotel that morning we said
goodbye...I was already in love with you...you know
that? In fact...my heart was probably yours before we
even left Señor Varez's bar,' Isabella told him, her upper
lip quivering slightly. 'Your stories about the Camino
and the way you told them enthralled me. Everything
about you just got to me...your looks, your voice, your
touch...they all filled me with such—such *yearning*
that I could hardly breathe. I went home and found both
to my consternation and joy that I was expecting your
baby. I gave birth to Raphael alone because I couldn't
even get in touch with you! I discovered that it was true
what I'd heard—that you guard your privacy as though
it were some untouchable, priceless work of art kept
behind steel walls...and the people who represent you
are only too happy to help you adhere to that.' Releasing
another shuddering breath, Isabella paused for a
moment as Leandro rolled to her side and stared up at
the ceiling. It was obvious that he didn't want to hear
what she was telling him, but she could not stop herself
from continuing. 'When I was pregnant with
Raphael...I learned what it was to have the *morriña* you
talk about descend. I was desolate without you... I
wondered how I would manage not even having the
hope of ever seeing you again. As Raphael started to
grow and every day he looked more and more like you
I knew it would be impossible to fall in love again with

somebody else. I resigned myself to a life of single par-
enthood and being a woman alone. Then you—then
you appeared at the library as if we'd only said goodbye
the day before. As if everything in your life had gone
nothing but right since we'd parted and maybe hoping
for a hot little repeat of what we'd shared in Spain—just
because you happened to be in London and thought
you'd make the most of the opportunity!'

Before Leandro could reply—to either protest or
defend himself—she pressed on...as if fearful that if she
stopped the flow of words that were pouring out, she
might never have the courage or opportunity to say them
again. 'Well...you found out about your son. You insisted
that you wanted to do the right thing and I had to come
to Spain with you and eventually be your wife. I discovered that your father got killed a month after we said
goodbye to each other and that your life had clearly *not*
gone completely right as I imagined it had when I saw
you. But still you refused to talk to me about him...to tell
me anything about your life other than scant anecdotes
that I could probably read in a gossip column if I so
chose! Even if you *did* love me, Leandro...how do you
think our marriage will work when you don't even trust
me enough to share your pain?'

Feeling the power of her words storm past his usual
defences and cut him to the bone, like a surgeon's
scalpel slicing through his flesh, Leandro put his hand
up to his throbbing temple and grimaced. 'You are right,
Isabella,' he admitted with stunning calm, even though
he hated himself right then for saying it. 'Everything
you say about me is true. But that is the way I am and,

even though you do not like it, I cannot change to be the man you want, simply because you wish me to. Now I have to get some sleep... I have only a couple of hours before I must get up and go to work.'

Saying no more, he threw back the covers on the bed, grabbed his jeans and pulled them on—then, without giving Isabella a backward glance, strode from the room and shut the door behind him...

CHAPTER ELEVEN

ISABELLA sat on the bed with Raphael playing with his rattle beside her and stared almost unseeingly at the neatly packed suitcase as though it belonged to a stranger and not her. Constanza had left a couple of hours ago, leaving enthusiastic promises in her wake to 'come back very soon', and Isabella had felt like the biggest deceiver of all time knowing that she and her son would not be there when she returned. She had arranged their clothes and belongings into her case like an automaton, not really registering what she was doing and unable to think about the future—hers and her little son's—without feeling as if she were being cut in two.

Would Leandro miss them even a little when they were gone? Isabella anguished. They had been part of his reality for such a short time, yet already she felt as though they'd spent whole lifetimes together. This morning, in the early hours when sleep had hardly touched her, she had heard Leandro come back into the bedroom. Pretending to be fast asleep, she had sensed him stand beside the bed next to where she lay and had heard him sigh deeply. It was hard not to believe that

that heartfelt release was one of regret. Regret that he had brought her to Spain and vowed to marry her when all he really wanted was his son.

He was unable to love her; that was clear now. Every time Isabella let the thought sink in, she wanted to die. Now…for better or worse…she had decided to return to England. As difficult and inconvenient as it might be for Leandro to have to make the trip to see Raphael, and as much as Isabella regretted forcing that scenario upon him, she could see no other alternative than make that decision for them both. It was simply inconceivable to even think of remaining here in Madrid with him under the circumstances, even though she'd partly convinced herself that she could. She had bared her soul to him last night and…and *nothing*. He was unmovable as far as his feelings were concerned. So…she would go home, try and make some proper time to finish writing her book about the Camino and work hard to achieve financial independence so that she might provide a decent future for her son. If Leandro wanted to contribute financially to his welfare, she would of course let him—but ultimately his demands were not going to override her own needs. She had allowed too many people in her life to do that to her in the past and Isabella wasn't about to let that happen again.

'Ouch!' She winced as Raphael's rattle hit her on the side of the head, then as she found him grinning back at her like the mischievous little cherub he was her heart melted as it always did where he was concerned. Lifting him onto her lap, she hugged him as if she would never let him go and pressed her lips tenderly into his sweet-smelling black hair…

* * *

Walking away from the set towards his trailer, Leandro briefly saluted the script editor engaged in conversation with one of his actors and called out to a catering assistant to bring him a cup of coffee. Inside the trailer, he moved to one of the padded leather wraparound seats and picked up the tabloid newspaper that he'd borrowed earlier from one of the extras he'd seen reading it. He and Isabella had made front-page news…

The picture that the shaven-headed paparazzo had taken stared back at him in unambiguous black and white and anyone with eyes to see could immediately detect that Leandro was very much enamoured of the stunning-looking girl he had clearly just been kissing. Longing, swift and biting, clutched at his heart. He did not need to stare at her picture to confirm how he *really* felt about Isabella. In fact he was almost ashamed of the way he had behaved with her last night, leaving her alone in their bed when she had so clearly needed him to respond lovingly to what she had told him—instead of getting up and moving to another room! All because he had not been able to relinquish the automatic urge to keep his feelings locked up tight behind those 'steel walls' that she had accused him of hiding behind. A habit that had—over time—developed into a strong belief that it was dangerous to let people get too close, that they might abuse or betray his trust if he let them.

The only person he had truly allowed to get close to him was his father. Even his mother Constanza had been kept at a distance much more than she deserved. If Leandro continued in this way, would he visit that reprehensible aloof behaviour even on Raphael…his own son? *Madre mia!* Isabella had already shared so much with him…her friendship, her loyalty *and* her body…and she had given him a child—a child she had borne alone because Leandro had been too wary of trusting her with his telephone number or even an address where she might write to him. Because he'd had a secret dread that she might elaborate on what had happened between them to her journalist sister and before he'd known it his delight in Isabella would have been trivialised and scandalised to appear in some careless magazine that would not have hesitated to tell the world what Leandro Reyes, 'famous director', had been up to!

Well…that had *not* happened. Isabella had obviously kept her word about not telling anyone else about their meeting in the Port of Vigo and he had heard nothing damning or scandalous about himself in any English publication. And in the meantime Leandro had paid the price for his foolishness and lack of trust and his son had lived the first nine months of his life not even knowing his father's touch… *Dios mio!* Such stupidity could not continue! If the feelings he had in his breast for Isabella were *not* those of passionate connection and love…then *what*, he would like to know, *were*?

Remembering the expression of sorrow on her face after she had told him that she loved him and he had not responded the same, Leandro rubbed an angry hand round his unshaven jaw and swore. He definitely should have spoken to her this morning before leaving for the film set…even though the hour had been early and he'd found her asleep. Now, he asked himself, what if she had taken his lack of communication as a sign that she was not welcome in his house any more? What if, right now, she was making her way to the airport? His stomach churned sickeningly in protest. Glancing down at his watch, Leandro calculated the time it would take him to drive home and back before he was due on set again to continue directing. Urgently needing to locate his assistant director and make his sudden plans known, he jumped to his feet and hurried from the trailer as though he'd just learned that somebody had put a bomb under it and it was about to be detonated…

Needing some fresh air and seduced by the honeyed golden sunshine that lit up the morning, despite the chilly breeze that was blowing, Isabella took Raphael outside with her to sit on the patio in a carved wooden rocking-chair. Tucking her cream woollen shawl around both of them as she fed her son his bottle of milk, she glanced towards the blue-grey horizon of hills that surrounded the *finca* and the undulating seam that divided them from the endless expanse of vivid azure sky. A cowbell over a doorway somewhere tinkled in the scented lilting air and Isabella momentarily closed her eyes to breathe in the evocative sound. A sound that helplessly nudged a still hurting bruise somewhere deep inside her.

When her lids opened again, a car was pulling up a few feet away from where she sat and she watched mesmerised as Leandro climbed out of the driver's seat and strolled commandingly towards her. Feeling as though she were watching a particularly arresting scene in a movie as her gaze flicked appreciatively over his long-legged denim clad stride, the waistband of his jeans riding low on his tight lean hips, and his charcoal grey T-shirt clinging to his undoubtedly muscular torso, Isabella held her breath for a moment in wonder. She could conjure up any number of gorgeous leading men from her favourite movies, but they would all pale into obscurity next to Leandro Reyes. The man would be box office dynamite if he chose to act as well as direct! But the fact that he was home in the middle of the day when she hadn't expected him was causing Isabella's heart to race for another reason. Had he returned to tell her that he realised that their marriage wouldn't work after all? Even though she'd packed her suitcase and written him a goodbye note, her mouth went dry.

'*Hola.*' His smile was in competition with the sun, it was so blindingly compelling. Why she was on the receiving end of such a dazzling gesture, Isabella couldn't guess, seeing as though relations between them last night had hardly concluded happily.

'Hi. Aren't you meant to be filming today?'

Sorrow and regret at her soon departure lingered in her blood like some debilitating malady but she managed to keep her tone level despite her distress.

'*Sí*…but I took some time off to come home for a little while.'

Stooping down beside them, Leandro planted a gentle kiss on Raphael's warmly rosy cheek. The baby stopped suckling the teat on his bottle and rewarded his father with a smile so sweet that now it was Leandro's turn to be dazzled.

'*Increíble,*' he murmured softly and could not resist

kissing his son again, letting the little boy wrap his tiny hand round his forefinger and hold it tight as he did so.

'He's pleased to see you,' Isabella commented lightly, wondering again *why* Leandro should want to take time off to come home, and secretly wishing that he would give her a little space so that she might resume normal, unhindered breathing. She didn't want to be at such a disadvantage with him...to find her composure shaken beyond rescue by the sight of those astonishing polished-slate eyes with their glossy sweeping lashes and the indelible warmth and scent of his incredibly smooth skin.

'And you, my lovely Isabella,' he replied disconcertingly, 'are *you* pleased to see me too?'

She thought about the packed suitcase she'd left on the bed, about the note she'd left him explaining why she couldn't stay...and then registered the astonishing endearment he'd addressed her with in confused surprise. 'I—' She tried desperately to find words but to her alarm none came readily.

'I think my father would have *adored* you.' Straightening to his full height, Leandro softly glanced his fingers against her hair. His action caused a swift electrical current to pulse through Isabella's insides, making her breasts ache and her thighs tremble. 'He would have said, "My son, you would be utterly foolish to let her go, because she is the *one*. No other woman will make you happy but her." He had very good judgement, my father. I trusted him implicitly.'

'What are you telling me, Leandro?'

'I am merely saying that—'

'Mama.'

Instantly diverted—they both stared down in mute amazement at their son, now wriggling to sit up in his mother's arms. Isabella glanced back up at Leandro, her dark eyes glistening. 'Did you hear him? Did you hear what he just said?' Squeezing the child to her fondly, she could have cried, her heart was so full. But now her son's wriggling turned into a definite struggle for freedom as he gazed up hopefully at his father. Smiling, Leandro put out his arms and the little boy went into them more than willingly. Leandro ruffled his curly hair and planted a resounding kiss on his soft cherubic cheek. They made an arresting picture, father and son, with their gleaming dark hair and striking good looks.

'I heard him, Isabella...but I am not surprised by his obvious intelligence. This little one will leave his mark on the world. I can feel it already. He is strong and he knows his own mind. Your "mama" is bewitching, is she not, Raphael?' He deliberately addressed the child. 'Can you wonder that I am crazy in love with her?'

'But you said—' Biting her lip, Isabella frowned in confusion, hardly daring to believe what her own ears were conveying to her. 'Why didn't you tell me that last night? How could you change your mind in such a short space of time?'

'Just because I am adept at directing films...does not mean that I am so adept in every other arena of my life.' Raising a self-deprecating eyebrow, Leandro further knocked Isabella off balance with a totally disarming grin. But then in the next instance his expression became almost sombre. 'In the past, I admit I have had a problem at knowing how to trust. People inevitably let us down from time to time and for some of us…it is almost *too* hard to learn how to give our trust again. When I started making films and began to get recognition for my work—I found it even *more* difficult to do that.

'Where relationships were concerned—how could I know that a woman liked me for myself or simply wanted to attach herself to me because of my name? In my industry particularly there is a definite tendency to have that happen. Even so…my father Vincente…he told me that I should not be so cautious…that there was no need to worry because I would absolutely know when the right woman for me came along…the one who would love me for myself and whom I would want to bear my children.

'He was *right*, Isabella. Why did I doubt that? I should have *known* as soon as you told me you were walking the Camino that we were kindred spirits. I should have known from the moment you walked into Señor Varez's bar and my heart missed a beat. This morning our picture from last night was in the paper. I gazed at your lovely face and I suddenly knew with the most stunning clarity how I felt about you. I did not even care that the paparazzi had taken the picture. I love you and I find myself wanting the world to know it! I am *proud* that you are the mother of this beautiful child that God has blessed us with…our son. Looking at both of you, I wonder how I will even survive the fear of anything untoward happening to either of you. Nothing is more precious to me than my family…you and Raphael. You will have to help me deal with this, Isabella.'

On trembling legs Isabella rose slowly to her feet.

Leaning across her beaming little son, she held Leandro's compelling face between her hands and kissed him almost feverishly. Uncaring that his hard and rough, unshaven jaw scraped against her more tender contours, she simply surrendered to the powerful need to show him how *much* she loved him and how she would willingly help him to trust and banish the fear of anything bad happening to any of them. Want and need poured through her veins with almost frightening demand as her lips cleaved lovingly to his. This man, this engaging, irresistible, fascinating storyteller—he was simply the love of her life. No other man would ever replace him, because no other man ever *could*.

'*Te amo, Leandro...te amo,*' she told him as she reluctantly came up for air.

'I see you have been working on your Spanish...very impressive.' He chuckled gently, shifting Raphael onto his hip and grasping Isabella's hand so that she could not escape their tender little circle. The look that blazed from his mercurial eyes was fierce with love. 'But I feel the need to help you improve by introducing you to some other equally delightful phrases that I would like to hear coming from your lips.'

'Oh?'

'*Sí*...such as, "When are you going to make love to me, Leandro, and can it be soon?"'

'Yes,' Isabella agreed quietly, helplessly blushing. 'That is *definitely* a phrase I need to know.'

* * *

Why was she taking so long? *Madre mia!* A man could go loco if he was required to be any more patient than he was being forced to be at the moment!

His mother had collected Raphael half an hour ago and their son would be spending the night with her so that Leandro and Isabella could enjoy some private time together. But instead of joining him in bed, as was his most ardent desire, Isabella had declared that she needed to freshen up first and had closeted herself in the bathroom to take a shower. Pacing the spacious bedroom for the umpteenth time, Leandro finally knocked impatiently on the bathroom door and—to his surprise—found it unlocked. The air was full of scented steam and as he called out Isabella's name and tried to make his voice heard above the rush of water from the shower his gaze cleaved helplessly to the provocative glimpse of smooth feminine flesh he had sighted behind the cubicle's glass door.

Every thought, emotion, sensation in Leandro's tautly muscled body seemed to flow straight to his groin. Almost rigid with near pain, he mentally pleaded for mercy. Opening the shower door, he was faced with his wife-to-be's 'innocent' and captivating smile as water cascaded liberally down over her glistening naked body. 'What took you so long?' she asked him, continuing to soap herself with a sponge as though not troubled by a single care.

'Dios!' Plucking the sponge from her hand, Leandro flung it away. 'You know you deserve to be punished for putting me through such excruciating torture, waiting for you when I could have been in here with you

all this time?' Shaking his head in disbelief and already barefoot, he dragged his shirt over his head and discarded it, then quickly did the same with his jeans and underwear.

'Oh?' Her dark eyes glowing with pleasure, Isabella stepped back to give him some room as he positioned his impressive physique beneath the cascading water and shut the door behind him. 'Should I be scared?'

'No.' He pressed his lips against hers in a wet, open-mouthed kiss that caused her to shudder violently with need. When he raised his head again he slid his hands down her body in hungrily urgent exploration. 'You should, however…get ready to moan and scream.'

'I don't know *what* you mean, Señor Reyes.' Teasing him as she gazed boldly up into his remarkably beautiful face—the sheen of the water highlighting his hard jaw and amazing cheekbones—Isabella shivered again beneath the steaming jet stream that sluiced down over her body.

'Then let me demonstrate…*sí*?'

Positioning his hands beneath her bottom, Leandro lifted her up and pressed her back against the shimmering aquamarine wall tiles as his lips got reacquainted with hers and he deftly and hotly inserted his rigid shaft into her moistly velvet centre. Feeling him fill her, then move inside her—his strength and need asserting his compelling male power—Isabella cried out, tears of joy sliding down her damp face as he ruthlessly possessed her, her heart aching fit to burst because she now knew that he loved her as much as she loved him.

She briefly reflected how her decision to walk the Camino Way had ultimately manifested in their meeting and she was in *awe* of the synchronistic events that had conspired to bring them together. Even Emilia—did she but know it—had played her part. There was definitely a certain irony in that. But now her attention was riveted by the passionate sensations that were flooding her body and she slid her hands over Leandro's tight, glistening biceps and revelled in the sheer depth of her love for him. His movements becoming more focused and urgent, his hard-muscled chest pinning her even more firmly to the slippery tiled wall—Isabella's senses exploded into delirium as she climaxed. Then she increased her grip on him—her arms firmly round his neck and her limbs weak and trembling from pleasure as she felt his body buck strongly beneath her. Her name was on his lips at the end of his own harshly voiced groan and Isabella smiled up into the dazed expression that had taken hold of his definitely captivating features.

'If that was meant to be punishment…just what do you do for *pleasure*, Señor Reyes?' she asked provocatively. Gently lowering her to the ground again, Leandro smoothed back her sodden dark hair either side of her face and surveyed her with almost solemn regard—as if this was not a matter to be taken at all lightly. 'We have a lifetime together as man and wife to find out…do we not, *mi angel*?' he said huskily.

MILLS & BOON®

Live the emotion

JANUARY 2007 HARDBACK TITLES

ROMANCE™

Royally Bedded, Regally Wedded *Julia James*	0 263 19556 2
The Sheikh's English Bride *Sharon Kendrick*	0 263 19557 0
Sicilian Husband, Blackmailed Bride *Kate Walker*	0 263 19558 9
At the Greek Boss's Bidding *Jane Porter*	0 263 19559 7
The Spaniard's Marriage Demand *Maggie Cox*	0 263 19560 0
The Prince's Convenient Bride *Robyn Donald*	0 263 19561 9
One-Night Baby *Susan Stephens*	0 263 19562 7
The Rich Man's Reluctant Mistress *Margaret Mayo*	
	0 263 19563 5
Cattle Rancher, Convenient Wife *Margaret Way*	0 263 19564 3
Barefoot Bride *Jessica Hart*	0 263 19565 1
Their Very Special Gift *Jackie Braun*	0 263 19566 X
Her Parenthood Assignment *Fiona Harper*	0 263 19567 8
The Maid and the Millionaire *Myrna Mackenzie*	0 263 19568 6
The Prince and the Nanny *Cara Colter*	0 263 19569 4
A Doctor Worth Waiting For *Margaret McDonagh*	0 263 19570 8
Her L.A. Knight *Lynne Marshall*	0 263 19571 6

HISTORICAL ROMANCE™

Innocence and Impropriety *Diane Gaston*	0 263 19748 4
Rogue's Widow, Gentleman's Wife *Helen Dickson*	0 263 19749 2
High Seas to High Society *Sophia James*	0 263 19750 6

MEDICAL ROMANCE™

A Father Beyond Compare *Alison Roberts*	0 263 19784 0
An Unexpected Proposal *Amy Andrews*	0 263 19785 9
Sheikh Surgeon, Surprise Bride *Josie Metcalfe*	0 263 19786 7
The Surgeon's Chosen Wife *Fiona Lowe*	0 263 19787 5

MILLS & BOON®   1206 Gen Std LP

Live the emotion

JANUARY 2007 LARGE PRINT TITLES

ROMANCE™

Mistress Bought and Paid For *Lynne Graham*	0 263 19415 9
The Scorsolini Marriage Bargain *Lucy Monroe*	0 263 19416 7
Stay Through the Night *Anne Mather*	0 263 19417 5
Bride of Desire *Sara Craven*	0 263 19418 3
Married Under the Italian Sun *Lucy Gordon*	0 263 19419 1
The Rebel Prince *Raye Morgan*	0 263 19420 5
Accepting the Boss's Proposal *Natasha Oakley*	0 263 19421 3
The Sheikh's Guarded Heart *Liz Fielding*	0 263 19422 1

HISTORICAL ROMANCE™

The Bride's Seduction *Louise Allen*	0 263 19379 9
A Scandalous Situation *Patricia Frances Rowell*	0 263 19380 2
The Warlord's Mistress *Juliet Landon*	0 263 19381 0

MEDICAL ROMANCE™

The Midwife's Special Delivery *Carol Marinelli*	0 263 19331 4
A Baby of His Own *Jennifer Taylor*	0 263 19332 2
A Nurse Worth Waiting For *Gill Sanderson*	0 263 19333 0
The London Doctor *Joanna Neil*	0 263 19334 9
Emergency in Alaska *Dianne Drake*	0 263 19531 7
Pregnant on Arrival *Fiona Lowe*	0 263 19532 5

MILLS & BOON®

Live the emotion

FEBRUARY 2007 HARDBACK TITLES

ROMANCE™

The Marriage Possession *Helen Bianchin*   978 0 263 19572 9
The Sheikh's Unwilling Wife *Sharon Kendrick*   978 0 263 19573 6
The Italian's Inexperienced Mistress *Lynne Graham*
                                                978 0 263 19574 3
The Sicilian's Virgin Bride *Sarah Morgan*   978 0 263 19575 0
The Rich Man's Bride *Catherine George*   978 0 263 19576 7
Wife by Contract, Mistress by Demand *Carole Mortimer*
                                                978 0 263 19577 4
Wife by Approval *Lee Wilkinson*   978 0 263 19578 1
The Sheikh's Ransomed Bride *Annie West*   978 0 263 19579 8
Raising the Rancher's Family *Patricia Thayer* 978 0 263 19580 4
Matrimony with His Majesty *Rebecca Winters*   978 0 263 19581 1
In the Heart of the Outback... *Barbara Hannay* 978 0 263 19582 8
Rescued: Mother-To-Be *Trish Wylie*   978 0 263 19583 5
The Sheikh's Reluctant Bride *Teresa Southwick*
                                                978 0 263 19584 2
Marriage for Baby *Melissa McClone*   978 0 263 19585 9
City Doctor, Country Bride *Abigail Gordon*   978 0 263 19586 6
The Emergency Doctor's Daughter *Lucy Clark*   978 0 263 19587 3

HISTORICAL ROMANCE™

A Most Unconventional Courtship *Louise Allen* 978 0 263 19751 8
A Worthy Gentleman *Anne Herries*   978 0 263 19752 5
Sold and Seduced *Michelle Styles*   978 0 263 19753 2

MEDICAL ROMANCE™

His Very Own Wife and Child *Caroline Anderson*
                                               978 0 263 19788 4
The Consultant's New-Found Family *Kate Hardy*
                                               978 0 263 19789 1
A Child to Care For *Dianne Drake*   978 0 263 19790 7
His Pregnant Nurse *Laura Iding*   978 0 263 19791 4

MILLS & BOON®

Live the emotion

0107 Gen Std LP

FEBRUARY 2007 LARGE PRINT TITLES

ROMANCE™

Purchased by the Billionaire *Helen Bianchin*	978 0 263 19423 4
Master of Pleasure *Penny Jordan*	978 0 263 19424 1
The Sultan's Virgin Bride *Sarah Morgan*	978 0 263 19425 8
Wanted: Mistress and Mother *Carol Marinelli*	978 0 263 19426 5
Promise of a Family *Jessica Steele*	978 0 263 19427 2
Wanted: Outback Wife *Ally Blake*	978 0 263 19428 9
Business Arrangement Bride *Jessica Hart*	978 0 263 19429 6
Long-Lost Father *Melissa James*	978 0 263 19430 2

HISTORICAL ROMANCE™

Mistaken Mistress *Margaret McPhee*	978 0 263 19382 4
The Inconvenient Duchess *Christine Merrill*	978 0 263 19383 1
Falcon's Desire *Denise Lynn*	978 0 263 19384 8

MEDICAL ROMANCE™

The Sicilian Doctor's Proposal *Sarah Morgan*	978 0 263 19335 0
The Firefighter's Fiancé *Kate Hardy*	978 0 263 19336 7
Emergency Baby *Alison Roberts*	978 0 263 19337 4
In His Special Care *Lucy Clark*	978 0 263 19338 1
Bride at Bay Hospital *Meredith Webber*	978 0 263 19533 0
The Flight Doctor's Engagement *Laura Iding*	978 0 263 19534 7